The Best Christmas Ever

By
Karin Ireland

CAREER PRESS
3 Tice Road
P.O. Box 687
Franklin Lakes, NJ 07417
1-800-CAREER-1
201-848-0310 (NJ and outside U.S.)
FAX: 201-848-1727

THE BEST CHRISTMAS EVER

ISBN 1-56414-198-5, $6.99

Cover design by Dean Johnson Design, Inc.

Printed in the U.S.A. by Book-mart Press

To order this title by mail, please include price as noted above, $2.50 handling per order, and $1.00 for each book ordered. Send to: Career Press, Inc., 3 Tice Road, P.O. Box 687, Franklin Lakes, NJ 07417.

Or call toll-free 1-800-CAREER-1 (Canada: 201-848-0310) to order using VISA or MasterCard, or for further information on books from Career Press.

Library of Congress Cataloging-in-Publication Data

Ireland, Karin.
    The best Christmas ever / by Karin Ireland.
       p.   cm.
    Includes bibliographical references (p.) and index.
    ISBN 1-56414-198-5 (pbk.)
    1. Christmas. I Title.
GT4985.I68   1995
394.2'663--dc20   95-24878
                                                   CIP

Dedication

This book is dedicated to Curt Rudick, who cooked a Christmas dinner for me when I was new in town. Thanks, Curt. Thanks also for all the interview coaching, the fun talks, the Mexican dinners and for endlessly rescuing me from computer crises. And thanks for being my friend.

Acknowledgments

I'd like to express a heartfelt thanks to all the people who helped me find the information I needed: Thank you, Jean Kest, Community Action Network; Lori Welle, Northwest Airlines; Catherine Soffin, Points of Light Foundation; Joan Bordow, The Holiday Project; A.T. Birmingham-Young, The Giraffe Project; Liz DeFranco, *Family*; Lisa J. Rodwell, *Woman's Day*; Jonatha Mathews, Borders Books and Music, Waikele; Rabbi Hal Libman, Jewish Federation of Hawaii; and Cheryl Bernstein.

My thanks go also to Ron Fry, Larry Wood and Betsy Sheldon at Career Press for letting me do this book and to Julie Castiglia, my agent and friend.

I feel like I can never thank my daughter Tricia enough for her literary insights and for her continued love and support. And I want to thank my parents, Bob and Anne, for their love and encouragement.

"Joy is not in things; it is in us."

Richard Wagner

Contents

How to capture the true spirit of the holidays

If you feel that there's something missing in your holidays, you're not alone. Most people struggle to keep peace from being crowded out by anxiety as they think of all the things they have to do by December 25. Love and joy may be replaced by frustration when you try to plan the perfect party or find the perfect gifts. Charity may seem impossible when you look at the balance in your bank account, and goodwill can give way to disappointment if your holidays turn out to be more commercial than spiritual.

It's possible to be stressed out with any holiday, but Christmas has become the most commercial, the most frantic and stressful and the hardest to enjoy.

Why? Because we want it to be perfect. Commercials warn us that if we don't buy the "right" ham, our dinner guests will run screaming from the table in search of almost anything else to eat. They scold that if we don't have the right wine, our guests will label us *gauche*. If we don't buy expensive gifts from the right stores, our friends won't know we really care.

While we're busy trying to do everything perfectly, it's easy to lose touch with the values we really want to honor. Values like joy, peace, patience, acceptance, charity and love.

As you read *The Best Christmas Ever,* you'll discover hundreds of ways you can create the holiday experience you want. You'll see how to shift the focus from commercial gifts to ones from the heart, how to slow down, do less, feel more, be more and enjoy more. You'll turn those stress-filled, exhaustive holidays into memories of the best Christmas ever.

❊ ❊ ❊

Live. Love. Laugh.

Notice wonders. Enjoy life. Have fun.

Chapter 1

How to find the perfect gift

...and enjoy the experience

"There are three arch-enemies of happiness: Hurry, Worry, and Debt."

Newell Dwight Hillis

What comes to mind when you think about holiday shopping? Crowds? Endless shopping trips that never result in the right gifts? Maxing out your credit cards?

Do you long for a way to inject more fun in the shopping experience? Do you wish you felt more holiday spirit and less like a project manager?

Cheer up, you're not alone. The good news is that it's not only possible, it's *easy* to find the perfect gift for everyone on your list and have fun at the same time. In the pages that follow, you'll discover dozens of ways you can find great gifts without spending all day or more money than you meant to. You'll learn about gifts that are friendly to the environment and others that help people who don't have much of their own. You'll read about gifts you can make and ways you can *be* the gift to family, friends and even strangers. There are also thoughts that will help you find balance between the things you want to do and the things you think you *should* do.

One of the most important secrets to recapturing the spirit and meaning of the holidays is to slow down so you can really experience and enjoy each moment. Savor the process as well as the result. Try not to rush through your gift shopping just to get it done. Make shopping a holiday celebration in itself—enjoy the decorations, plan a nice dinner with a friend after a day-long outing, buy yourself a little gift.

Another key to successful shopping: Try not to get caught up in questions like, "Does it look like I've spent enough?" and "How do I know he/she will like it?" The answer is—you can't know the answer to either question. But then, that's not what the spirit of the holidays is about. The holidays are about *giving*.

଼ ଼

The best tip about shopping with little kids is...don't. Hire a sitter. Trade time with another parent. Bribe a sibling to stay home with the little ones, or, as a last resort, to go along and be responsible for them.

Still, if you must shop with them in tow here are some things you can do to shift the possibility of success in your favor:

- ◆ Shop early in the morning when everyone (including the sales staff) is rested.
- ◆ Bring snacks for small shoppers. Bring snacks for big shoppers, too.
- ◆ Compliment little ones for their patience and their good behavior.
- ◆ Keep the shopping trip short.
- ◆ Don't expect kids to have more patience with shopping than you have with them.
- ◆ Don't insist that reluctant children visit Santa.

- ◆ Dangle carrots. The promise of an ice cream after the shopping trip "if everybody's happy" has brought clarity to many toddlers who momentarily lose focus. Also, asking, "Is everybody happy?" in a doubtful tone usually works as a reminder and it makes a much better impression on fellow shoppers than snarling, "If you don't stop that this instant, I'm going to strangle you."

- ◆ Encourage your kids to hint about what they want (usually that's not at all difficult) and then cut your shopping time to a fraction by calling stores ahead of time and asking them to hold the item for you. Consider choosing only one or two large gifts per child and then some smaller ones just for the fun of having things to open. It's easy to get carried away, but you can't possibly buy them enough to show them how much you love them. And if you buy too many big gifts, each one will be less appreciated.

"There is more to life than increasing its speed."

Mahatma Gandhi

Look for ways to make holiday shopping *easier* (and more fun!) than it was last year. Take a vacation day from work to shop. Make a list of everyone you want to buy for and go to an area of town where you think you'll have the most success.

Take a large shopping bag with you to put your purchases in. It's easier not to have to keep track of a dozen little bags and it's better for the environment if you don't have a dozen paper or plastic bags to throw away as soon as you get home. If you use a beach tote, it won't rip and you can zip it up.

≈೦ ೧≋

Here are two things I've learned the hard way: 1) You don't have to lug your whole purse along if you tuck the necessities in the bottom of a shopping bag; and 2) it's more important to wear shoes that are comfortable than ones that match your outfit.

≈೦ ೧≋

Some people are hard to shop for, but that's no reason to let frustration overwhelm your good intentions. If you're shopping for someone who is generally hard to please, don't take it personally. And don't think that if you try harder, this year you'll finally find the gift that makes him or her dance with joy. Realize that you can only control the *giving* part of the act, not the way it will be received. Someone who has seemed ungrateful in the past will probably seem ungrateful no matter what you give. Choose something that's nice but simple.

* * *

For people on your list who are gracious recipients but nevertheless difficult to buy for, think about their hobbies, wishes, fantasies. Look for books, music or games that have something to do with these interests but don't make it a chore. If you're stumped, try one of these:

- ♦ *Life Smiles Back,* Philip B. Kunhardt, Jr. More than 200 classic humorous photos from the famous back page of *Life* magazine. $14.

- ♦ *A Day in the Life of America.* Dozens of photographers took pictures of people across America all on one day. $45. Other *A Day in the Life* books are available about Australia, the Soviet Union, Spain (in English and Spanish), Canada, Italy, Ireland, Japan (in English and Japanese) and Hawaii.

♦ *Brother Wolf, a Forgotten Promise,* Jim Brandenburg. In this award-winning book, the beautifully told story of wolves is accompanied by incredible photographs the author took, seemingly from the vantage point of another wolf. $40.

♦ *Juggling for the Complete Klutz,* John Cassidy and B.C. Rimbeau. This book comes complete with instructions for beginners and three soft blocks to juggle. Also available is *The Klutz Yo-Yo Book.* $10.95.

♦ *555 Ways to Put More Fun in Your Life,* Bob Basso, Ph.D. $6.95.

❈ ❈ ❈

Seniors can be a challenge to find gifts for because it seems like they already have everything! The trick is to look for items that they use up and need to replace, or items that make life easier for them. For example:

♦ Fragrant body lotion or powder.
♦ Remote-control devices with very large switching buttons.
♦ Large-print books.
♦ Books on tape.
♦ A gift certificate for a manicure or pedicure.
♦ Snugly slippers.
♦ Lunch or dinner at a favorite restaurant.
♦ A picture of you in a pretty frame.
♦ A stuffed animal to sleep with.

ℰ ℭ

There's always the dilemma of whether casual friends or co-workers will give you a gift. If they don't, it could be awkward to give *them* something. On the other hand, if they *do* give you a gift, it could be awkward not to have something to give back. One option is to give something handmade—cookies, candies, jellies—and wrap it in plastic wrap rather than gift paper.

Another way to avoid embarrassment is to buy something you would enjoy having—a music tape or CD, a box of nice note cards, a fun calendar, a vintage magazine from a used bookstore. Wrap it, and wait to see if the gift exchange happens. If it does, you're prepared. If it doesn't, unwrap the gift and enjoy it yourself.

ℰℴ ℭℛ

To solve the dilemma of what to give a business associate, consider making a donation to charity in the recipient's name. While it wouldn't be the best choice for someone who would rather receive a personal gift, it's becoming a popular way for employees of one company to thank employees of another company for a business relationship— more appreciated than another fruit cake or cheese log, and more likely to conform to company rules.

ℰℴ ℭℛ

If you're looking for ways to express the holiday spirit by giving, chances are your co-workers are, too. Why not take up a collection from your department and make a contribution to your local Ronald McDonald House, a shelter for the homeless or a charity that has special meaning to one of your co-workers? Organize a packaged food drive and call a local church or social welfare office to find a good recipient. Or get the whole company together for a collection of Toys for Tots. Call your local Marine Reserve office for information.

"Never doubt that a small group of thoughtful, committed citizens can change the world; indeed, it's the only thing that ever has."

Margaret Meade

Think twice before surprising someone with a pet as a gift. Pets require attention and care and some live a very long life. Some recipients may not be willing or able to devote the time and care that a pet needs and deserves.

Other gifts that deserve a second thought are alcohol, candies (who isn't watching cholesterol these days?) and incense, scented candles and potpourri (people with asthma and other respiratory sensitivities can have a bad reaction).

℘ ℭ
....

"Mallphobia." The definition could be the fear of large buildings that display a bewildering array of gifts that all cost too much and that are all being looked at by too many jostling people. Some shoppers have found the antidote to mallphobia is to do their holiday shopping in October or early November, and others have found great satisfaction not going to a mall at all.

Here are nearly a dozen places to find great gifts without going near the mall:

♦ Plant nurseries.
♦ Antique stores.
♦ Street fairs.
♦ Craft shops and church bazaars.
♦ Yard sales.
♦ Flea markets.
♦ Hardware stores.
♦ Ice cream shops, coffee bars, restaurants, movie theaters, bookstores, beauty shops, massage therapists and anyplace else that offers gift certificates.
♦ Magazine stands. If you're late, send in the subscription and mail a gift card directly to the recipient to let them know it's coming.
♦ Mail-order companies.

୨୦ ୧୨

Speaking of mail-order, there are hundreds of reputable companies that offer wonderful gifts you can purchase right from your home. Order as early as possible if it's for a specific date, photocopy your order (including company name, address and phone number) if you can and save the copy for your records. Generally, credit card orders are processed more quickly than orders that are paid for by check. When you call to request a catalog, ask how long it will take to be delivered and how quickly your orders will be shipped. (If you're in a rush, most mail-order firms will mail the gift to your recipient.) Some companies have 24-hour operators, seven days a week.

Here are some companies that are popular with couch shoppers:

- *Hammacher Schlemmer.* In addition to state-of-the-art electronic gifts, the catalog of this 147-year-old company offers selections that are unique (Bungee Bouncer™ Trampoline System) and luxurious (full-body feather pillow). (800) 543-3366. For incentives/corporate gifts, call John Wynn at (312) 649-7362.

- *Tiffany & Company.* Tiffany offers several catalogs of elegant gifts that include silver candle holders, goblets, dinnerware, baby gifts, crystal, silver and gold jewelry. Call (800) 526-0649. For a catalog of business selections call (800) 423-2394.

- *Miles Kimball.* For 60 years, this company has offered items you didn't know you needed until you saw them in this catalog. Many are designed to make life easier (under-the-bed storage baskets), more comfortable (foil steering-wheel covers for when your car is parked in the hot sun) or more fun (woolly lamb lawn sheep). (414) 231-4886.

- *Neiman Marcus.* Elegant fine clothes for casual, office and evening wear. Custom gift-wrapping and Federal Express overnight shipping are available. (800) 825-8000.

- *Karen's Creme Classiques.* A tempting selection of decadent cakes, beautifully wrapped to suit any occasion, shipped by priority mail anywhere in the U.S. Average price is $29. These cakes make good personal as well as company gifts. For information, write Dan Cupp, Karen's Creme Classiques, 31921 Camino Capistrano, Suite 120, San Juan Capistrano, CA 92675 or call (714) 443-1919.

- *Windsor Vineyards.* One of the country's most awarded wineries offers a wide variety of its award-winning California wines with your message of up to three lines printed right on the label. Currently available in 11 states, these wines are marketed as corporate gifts but are also available, in case lots, to private buyers. Call David Rote, (800) 234-9046.

- *The Metropolitan Museum of Art.* This company has more than a dozen retail stores, and the catalog represents the products available there. Gifts, each a reproduction of museum art, include Russian jewelry, 17th-century silver Dutch boxes, art books and stationery. (800) 468-7386.

- *Starbucks Coffee Company.* Like the popular coffee house itself, the mail-order division offers the finest coffee around the globe plus coffee accessories. Starbucks works in partnership with CARE to provide development aid to people in coffee-producing countries like Guatemala, Ethiopia and Kenya. (800) 445-3428.

- *The National Wildlife Federation.* The federation's goal is to educate, inspire and help people and organizations conserve wildlife. It contributes 10 to 15 percent of the price of its catalog items to support conservation education programs. Catalog items include jewelry and clothing, blankets, bird feeders, Christmas cards and nature games. (800) 432-6564.

- *Exposures, A Whole New Way to Look at Pictures.* This company specializes in frames, calendars, albums and other ways to display photographs. (800) 222-4947.

- *The Horchow Collection* and the *Horchow Home Collection*. Unique home wares that range from cactus muffin tins to bright-colored pottery and fine china to linen and personalized stationery and furniture. Federal Express overnight shipping is available. (800) 456-7000.
- *Trifles.* Unique gifts for the home and patio include Monet "Boats" beach towels, oriental and museum-type decorator pieces. Federal Express overnight shipping is available. (800) 456-7019.
- *Orvis.* This 140-year-old company has more than a dozen catalogs, each for a specific market: clothing (mostly vacation/country clothing) and gifts, (800) 541-3541; fishing and outdoor, (800) 548-9548; Orvis travel (luggage and vacation clothing), (800) 541-3541; hunting and fishing (clothing and equipment), (800) 548-9548; Orvis fly-tying materials and rod building, (800) 548-9548.

ℰ ℂ

If you *do* go the mall, here are some ways to make it less stressful. In rural and suburban areas, shop on the way home from work when most people will go home for dinner. In the city, try shopping on weekends when most of the working crowds are gone.

If you drive to the mall when it's crowded, it's worth a few dollars to take advantage of a valet service if available. Then after you've finished shopping you can relax at the curb while *they* try to find your car.

Ask about the services of personal shoppers at large department stores. Because the shoppers are familiar with the merchandise, they'll know where to look for the items you want. The gifts don't have to be expensive to use the service and usually the service is free.

ℰ ℂ

Books make wonderful gifts that can be enjoyed over and over again, and some bookstores boast couches and espresso bars where you can take a leisurely look at things that interest you. How much easier could they *make* it?

Here are some of my favorite books for inspiration and fun:

- ◆ *101 Ways to Enjoy Life's Simple Pleasures*, Donna Watson, Ph.D., $7.95.
- ◆ *Wonderful Ways to Love a Child*, Judy Ford. A wonderful guide for parents who want to put love into action. $9.95.
- ◆ *Life's Little Instruction Book: 511 Suggestions, Observations, and Reminders on How to Live a Happy and Rewarding Life*, H. Jackson Brown, Jr. $9.95.
- ◆ *301 Random Acts of Kindness: A User's Guide to a Giving Life*, Mary K. Colf and Len Oszustowicz. $7.95.
- ◆ *A Year of Kindness: 365 Ways to Spread Sunshine*, Hanoch McCarty and Meladee McCarty, $8.95.
- ◆ *Don't Squat With Yer Spurs On: A Cowboy's Guide to Life*, Texas Bix Bender. Humorous observations that apply to people who don't wear spurs, too. $5.95.
- ◆ *New Shoes*, Jeff MacNelly. More fun adventures of the *Shoe* comic strip characters. $7.95.
- ◆ *Simplify Your Life: 100 Ways to Slow Down and Enjoy the Things That Really Matter*, Elaine St. James. $6.95.
- ◆ *Really Important Stuff My Kids Have Taught Me*, Cynthia Copeland Lewis. $6.95.
- ◆ *14,000 Things to Be Happy About*, Barbara Ann Kipfer. $6.95.
- ◆ *The Quotable Woman: Witty, Poignant, and Insightful Observations from Notable Women*. $12.95.
- ◆ *Illusions: The Adventures of a Reluctant Messiah*, Richard Bach. $ 18.95 hardcover, $5.99 paperback.
- ◆ *Creative Visualization*, Shakti Gawain. $9.95

ℰℴ ℂℛ
....

In recent years several stores have appeared, offering gifts that encourage kids (and grown-up kids) to think and explore, gifts that encourage curiosity or that help explain the universe. These make good alternatives to toys that are all flash and no substance.

Imaginarium is a child-friendly store with a commitment to "only sell nonviolent toys that promote learning and creativity." The store carries a good selection of children's books, art supplies, craft and science kits, collector dolls, Brio train sets, puzzles, puppets and games and activities that encourage kids to think, imagine and explore.

Imaginarium also carries a selection of award-winning educational software titles. About one-third of the Imaginarium stores have computer stations where customers of all ages can try out the software titles that are available for purchase. To find one of the 68 stores nearest you, call (800) 765-8697 or look in your telephone book.

* * *

Learningsmith, A General Store for the Curious Mind, is another toy store for young and old that is devoted to products that encourage curiosity and learning. It features games, books, computer software, craft sets and science activities for all ages. Look for them in your telephone book or call information.

* * *

Natural Wonders is a gift store mostly for grownups that specializes in gentle gifts like hand-crafted jewelry, books on nature, wind chimes, bird feeders, kaleidoscopes, coffee-table gift books on nature, tapes and hiking accessories. But my daughter reminds me that there are also many fun and educational toys for kids from computer and space exploration to toys that make strange noises and flash colored lights when you touch them. To find the store closest to you, call (800) 2-WONDER.

....

ℰℒ ℭℛ

If there's a blessing to the economic crunch, it's that people understand the importance of not spending more than they have. People are beginning to recognize that how much money they have or are willing to spend is not a measure of their success or love. Here are some tips on how you can spend less:

- Pay cash—it forces you to pay attention when you spend it.
- If you must use credit cards, only use one and use the one with the lowest credit level and interest rate.
- Plan ahead—set a limit on how much you plan to spend and stick to it. Don't be tempted to buy "just one more little thing."
- Shop early in the season or shop at the last minute if you prefer. Try not to do both, because you'll tend to buy and spend more.
- Carry a small notepad and write down every penny you spend the entire month of December. Transfer the total to a notebook every night.
- Don't let emotion (love, guilt, frustration) spend your money. Don't buy gifts to make things better.
- Stay out of pricey stores.
- Think of food, craft or service gifts you can give.
- Shop at yard sales and flea markets.
- If you're part of a large family, consider drawing names. Anyone who still wants to give to everyone can, but the obligation would be gone.

ℰℒ ℭℛ

Here are some gift ideas that are less commercial and good for your budget:

- Plant cuttings. Pot them and add a fancy bow.

♦ Baked cookies or candies. Find a great old dish or bowl at a thrift shop or yard sale to put them in. Include the recipe on a 3 x 5 card.
♦ Gifts from yard sales, flea markets, bazaars.
♦ Music tapes or CDs. Or put together a selection of favorites yourself.
♦ Coupon books with pledges of treats and services (by you).

For friends:

♦ Baby-sitting.
♦ A casserole, ready to heat and serve.
♦ Driving an extra day in the carpool.
♦ A special dessert for a celebration or party.
♦ Taking care of animals and/or plants when they go away.
♦ A picnic in your favorite park or place in the country.

For someone special:

♦ Back rubs.
♦ Special dinner, with candles.
♦ Bubble baths, with candles.
♦ A break from the kids, in-laws, telephone, home cooking.

For kids:

♦ Trips to the ice-cream shop.
♦ A favorite meal, on demand.
♦ A later bedtime.
♦ A ride, on demand. Okay, an *extra* ride, on demand.
♦ Being excused from doing a chore.
♦ Breakfast in bed.
♦ Not having to clean his or her room for a week.

"Teach us to delight in simple things."

Rudyard Kipling

Other great gifts for kids are books. They provide questions and answers, adventures and just plain fun. As an extra bonus, many of the books listed here give the reader and listener an opportunity to be together.

Here are more than a dozen books for young children that grown-ups will enjoy too:

♦ *Mama, Do You Love Me?*, by Barbara M. Joosse and beautifully illustrated by Barbara Lavallee. A young arctic child asks a series of what-if questions to test the limits of her mother's love. $13.95.

♦ *The Legend of the Bluebonnet*, Tomie DePaola. The story of a young Comanche's sacrifice to save her people from continued drought and famine. Paper, $5.95, hardcover, $14.95.

♦ *Helga's Dowry*, Tomie DePaola. A young troll girl takes responsibility for earning her own dowry and is rewarded for her integrity. Paper, $4.95, hardcover, $15.95.

♦ *Brown Angels*, by Walter Dean Myers. A collection of poems and charming turn-of-the-century photographs of African-American children. $16.

♦ *My First Word Book*, Angela Wilkes. A wonderful variety of colorful crisp photos on hundreds of subjects that include clothes, pets, toys, tools, sports, positions, opposites, things in the home, kitchen, bathroom, at the zoo and at school. Not your average word book. $12.95.

♦ *Lives of the Musicians: Good Times, Bad Times (And What the Neighbors Thought)*, Kathleen Krull. Written for children, but this would be a fun gift for music-loving grownups, too. $18.95.

- *Beethoven Lives Upstairs,* Barbara Nichol. Great insight into the life of Ludwig von Beethoven told through letters between the young boy who must share his home with this "madman" tenant and the boy's uncle, who encourages his nephew to be understanding of this odd but brilliant man. This is another music book written for children that would be a fun gift for music-loving grownups, too. $15.95. (This story comes on cassette tape, and some of Beethoven's more popular music is woven between the child and the uncle reading their letters aloud.)
- *When I Get Bigger,* Mercer Mayer. Little Critter looks forward to all the things he'll do when he's bigger, but right now he's got to go to bed because his parents say he isn't bigger yet. A fun book for young children. Large format paperback, $2.25.
- A *Kiss for Little Bear,* Else Holmelund Minarik, illustrated by Maurice Sendak. This I-Can-Read book tells about the picture Little Bear sends to his grandmother via his friends and the kiss she sends back—the same way. Other Little Bear titles include *Little Bear, Little Bear's Friend, Father Bear Comes Home,* and *Little Bear's Visit.* $3.50 paperback, $14 hardcover.
- *Grandfather's Journey,* written and illustrated with beautiful paintings by Allen Say. A simple story that recounts his grandfather's move as a young man from Japan to America, $16.95.
- *Time for Bed,* Mem Fox. Story in rhyme as animal mamas say goodnight to their little ones. The last one is a human mama and her child. Beautiful illustrations by Jane Dyer. For young children, $13.95.
- *The Dragons are Singing Tonight,* Jack Prelutsky. Fun poems for dragon lovers, $15.
- *Tales from the African Plains,* retold by Anne Gatti, paintings in vivid color by Gregory Alexander, $18.99.

හ ආ

....

Do you ever get the urge to *make* your gifts? Do you ever follow that thought with, "Nah, I can't because..." Well, here are some gifts you *can* make even if you don't have much time or talent:

♦ Potpourri. Common ingredients include cinnamon sticks, orange peel, dried flowers, tiny tree cones and evergreen sprigs. Here's how to make it: Dry thin slices of orange peel in a warm place. When dried, put them in a jar and shake with the other ingredients. Leave the jar closed for eight weeks if you have that much time, and shake it daily. When it's ready, put a tablespoon or two of the blend in a square of colorful fabric and tie with a ribbon or put a handful of the potpourri in a small gift bowl and cover with plastic wrap and a bow.

♦ Herb basting brush. Select branches of dried herbs, tie them with fine string to the ends of chopsticks to create a brush.

♦ Orange pomander. Stick rows of cloves into oranges, limes or kumquats. Wrap a silky ribbon around the fruit which can be hung as a decoration.

♦ Bath tray. Find a wooden bathtub tray at a bath shop, fill it with soaps, a loofah, bubble bath and bath salts.

♦ Gift basket. Create a gift basket with jams and jellies, wild rice mixes, flavored coffees or teas, spices and condiments.

♦ Stationery. Buy paper and enclose some pretty stamps.

♦ Neck pillow. Cut off the leg of a pair of children's pants. Hem the cut end, stuff, then fasten both ends with ribbon, yarn or colored rubber bands.

හ ආ

....

If you're concerned that your kids are missing out on the true spirit of the holidays, you're not alone. Unless you've hidden them on a

....

remote island someplace away from malls and television, there's no way they can avoid repeated messages of "buy and get."

You can minimize their exposure to the "gimmies" by limiting TV time during the sales frenzy periods. There are ways to counter the commercialism they *are* exposed to with messages of sharing, giving and thankfulness.

For example, ask children, "What are you planning to *give?*" rather than "What do you want to *get?*"

* * *

During December, let your kids each have a wish jar to keep in the kitchen or living room. Tell them that whenever they think of something they really want, rather than begging *you* for it, they should write it on a piece of paper and put it in their wish jar. Every day or two they should go through the wish jar and throw away any requests that are no longer top choices. Let them know the date of the last wishing day.

* * *

In addition to wishes for toys, encourage them to include wishes for things like the good health of a family member, success of a friend, an end to hate, hunger and homelessness.

* * *

Here's another way to help your kids focus on giving rather than getting. Put a "coin can" (a soda can works if you enlarge the hole) on the kitchen counter and encourage everyone in the family to contribute change. When it's full, count it—you'll be surprised how much there is—and then have a family meeting to choose a charity to donate it to.

* * *

Adopt a family in your town and spend some of your normal holiday gift money to help them. If you don't know a family who needs help, you might find one through a local church, school, shelter or community group. If you'd like to make the donations anonymous, ask a minister or teacher to make the delivery or send a cashier's check in a nice card.

❋ ❋ ❋

When your kids go grocery shopping with you, let them choose one or two canned items to add to a Christmas food bag. Keep the bag out in the kitchen where everybody can see it and when it's full, donate it to a needy family or a charity.

❋ ❋ ❋

Teach children about giving by suggesting there may be toys he or she has outgrown that a less fortunate child would enjoy having. This isn't the time to teach sacrifice (life will offer opportunities for that lesson) by insisting he or she give something that's a favorite.

§‍○ ○‍§

Kids seem to be the only ones with time on their hands during the holidays. So why not let them put their time and talent to making your holiday cards and wrapping paper? Blank cards are available at most stationery stores and shelf paper makes good wrapping paper. Kids can decorate the paper by using stamps carved from a sliced raw potato, a sponge or a cork. For ink, use colored ink or poster paint. For a textured look, try dipping one half of the sponge stamp in one color paint and the other half in a different color. Another idea is to cut a design out of a 3 x 5 card and use it as a stencil. Use colored pens and a sweeping motion to transfer the design to the paper. Or they can use finger paints and create designs by hand.

§‍○ ○‍§

If your kids are willing to make gifts, too, here are some they can do with little or no supervision:

♦ Custom-painted photo frames are one-of-a-kind. Buy glossy painted wooden frames, decorate them with painted designs and, if you're giving them to a relative, put in a photo of the family.

- A draft snake keeps drafts from coming in under doors. Choose a fun pattern of material, cut a rectangle about 10 inches wide and about four inches longer than the width of a door. Fold the cloth lengthwise, inside out, and sew small stitches on the long side and one end. Turn the material right side out, stuff with sand or rice. Sew the opening closed. Stitch on buttons for eyes if you want to.

- Newspaper logs are perfect for someone with a fireplace. You'll need lots of newspapers, a 2½ foot dowel and some string. Take a section of newspaper and remove any paper with colored ink (which can be toxic when burned). Put a section in front of you, put a dowel at the bottom, tightly roll about three inches of paper around the dowel. Then slide another section of newspaper over the end of the first one and continue to roll tightly. Repeat this step until you have a log the thickness you want. Tie the twine and pull the dowel out.

- A bird treat is a great gift for nature lovers. Buy a loaf of unsliced French bread, whisk an egg and brush generously over the bread, sprinkle with wild bird seeds or sesame seeds. Bake a few minutes to set the seeds. Then leave it, uncovered, on a rack for 24 hours. Poke a piece of bright-colored ribbon or yarn through one end with an ice pick or small knife, leave a big enough loop for hanging, and tie on a pretty bow.

℘ ℘

If you're looking for gifts that are friendly to Mother Earth, choose things that are long-lasting rather than disposable, items that tend to be passed along to others rather than thrown out, gifts that are recyclable or biodegradable, foods that are consumed. For example:

- Food gifts: cookies, cakes, special breads.
- Rechargeable batteries and recharger.

- Potted plants.
- Stationery made from recycled paper.
- Bird feeders.
- Fountain pens.
- Wooden toys.
- Solar-powered electronics (e.g. personal stereo, calculator).
- Hardcover books.
- Stamp-collecting kits.
- Stuffed animals.
- Potpourri.
- Gifts without excessive packaging.
- Burlap shopping bags.

⋙ ⋘

And then there are ecologically correct wrapping and packing materials:

- A basket or container that's already been used. Add a flower and a spray of greenery.
- Wrapping paper that's been recycled.
- Brown grocery bag paper, stenciled with holiday designs.
- Unwaxed white paper, stenciled with a holiday design.
- Red and green yarn to fasten packages instead of costly plastic-coated ribbon.
- Recycled boxes for shipping.
- Newspapers to cushion packages you mail.
- Reused ribbon and bows.
- Gift tags made with brown bag paper and stencils.

❈ ❈ ❈

If you receive packages with bubble wrap or plastic "peanuts," donate them to a mailing center like Mail Boxes, Etc. for reuse.

৪১ ৫৪

What are gifts you'd like for yourself this holiday season? Peace, calm, contentment, joy and love? If you will spend as much time and effort finding ways to have these gifts for yourself as you spend looking for gifts for others, you'll be amazed at the results. If you need to justify taking time for yourself, know that when you're peaceful, calm and contented, you not only *have* a gift, you *are* a gift.

Give yourself the gifts of:

♦ Family. Slow down, be with them, listen to them, talk on the phone to people you can't be with, enjoy pleasant memories of family you can't call.
♦ Friends. Take the time to get together for lunch, dinner or a quiet talk.
♦ Good health. Take time to eat balanced meals, exercise, meditate, walk, listen to music you enjoy.
♦ Spiritual connection. If you recognize a higher power in whatever form, take time to explore the meaning of that connection and ways you can express your highest ideals.
♦ Peace. Don't expect yourself to be perfect. Do your best every day and applaud yourself for doing that.
♦ Safety. If you're in a relationship in your personal or work life that is unsafe, leave. If you're uncertain about the urgency of leaving, talk to a trusted friend, a member of the clergy (it doesn't have to be one you know), or your local police department non-emergency number for referrals. Get guidance, learn your options, take care of yourself.

৪১ ৫৪

Love is a gift and, like other gifts, has to be *given* to be appreciated. Sometimes we listen to the messages our ego shouts—what we have to accomplish and how that has to look—rather than to the quieter messages from our hearts. When we let ourselves become rushed by trying to do too much, we often forget to show our love in the simplest ways. Look for ways to *be* the gift.

- Every morning ask yourself, "Whose life can I make brighter today?"
- Take extra time to listen to people who want and need to talk to you; take time to read an extra story at bedtime or in the middle of the day, just because. Borrow books from the library and read to your children every night.
- Look for opportunities to say yes, praise, congratulate, compliment, encourage and support others.
- Look for opportunities to be loving, gentle, compassionate, caring, generous and forgiving.
- Give gifts of praise, support, encouragement, confidence, and hugs.

"Kind words can be short and easy to speak, but their echoes are truly endless."

Mother Teresa

- Display your child's art and gifts proudly.
- Smile a lot, especially at children and old people.
- Write a Christmas letter to all the people in your family and let them know all the things you love about them.
- Send love notes in backpacks and lunch boxes, hide them on pillows, in shirt pockets and shoes.
- Take your kids to a park they've never been to before. Take along a new book for you.
- Slow down. It's hard to be patient, kind and loving when you're moving at the speed of sound.

♦ If you're divorced, give your children the gift of their other parent. Avoid talking badly about him or her. Don't prohibit or sabotage visits. Support your children if they want to buy or make a gift for their other parent.

♦ Let others be in the limelight. If someone else has captured the group's attention with a humorous story or nostalgic anecdote, avoid the temptation to tell of a time when you did just the same thing.

♦ Take time to notice who in your community needs help, and do what you can.

♦ Visit someone at a nursing home who doesn't have visitors. Take a small Christmas or Hanukkah gift. Some of these residents are confined to bed all day with no breaks in their routines, no one to talk to, no expectation of anything new in their lives—ever. Call the nurses ahead to find a good candidate.

♦ Offer to take someone who is homebound holiday shopping.

♦ Invite college students who won't be going home for the holidays to celebrate with you.

♦ Sprinkle packets of wildflowers where others will enjoy them.

♦ Volunteer to be a literacy tutor and give someone the gift of books. Many adult nonreaders are bright men and women who bluffed their way through school and life. Agencies generally request a commitment of 50 total hours, which amounts to one hour a week for a year, or two hours a week for six months. Contact your local library or church for information on literacy groups and training, or call the National Literacy Hotline at (800) 228-8813, Literacy Volunteers of America National Headquarters, (315) 445-8000 or C.O.R.E. at (800) 626-4601.

♦ Every day in December, say a quick prayer for someone who's not well. Say a prayer when an ambulance passes. Say a prayer for the hurt, the hungry, the homeless.

- Support businesses that support the community. Many offer jobs to wonderful people who, because of age, mental or physical challenges, are turned away by other companies. Support businesses that donate a percentage of their profits to charity.

- Volunteer to be a Big Brother or Big Sister. Big Brothers/Big Sisters matches volunteer men and women with boys and girls who are being raised in group homes or by single parents. The goal of the program is for the Big Brother or Sister to become a positive role model who provides some guidance and lots of encouragement and friendship. Generally, the commitment requested is for one year (so you'll be able to share the next holiday season with him or her), spending three to six hours with the child each week. Look for Big Brothers/Big Sisters in your phone directory.

"Charity sees the need, not the cause."

German Proverb

- Get your car washed by kids who are doing it as part of a fund-raising event.
- Participate in a charity walk or run.
- If you can afford to, give something to a homeless person each day in December.
- Take a few minutes every day to be thankful for what you have.
- Take cookies or donuts to your local firefighters on Christmas, just to thank them for being there.
- Write letters to servicemen and women who will be away from home during the holidays.

- Donate used eyeglasses to the Lions Clubs International. These glasses will be repaired, if needed, and distributed to others in need. Look for collection boxes in places like banks, restaurants, YMCA/YWCA lobbies, or consult your telephone book for a Lions Clubs listing.
- Carry an organ donor card.
- Donate nice household items, clothes and everything else you don't need to the Salvation Army, Goodwill or a church that plays Santa to the community. Not only will they make great gifts, but having less "stuff" to care about gives you more time to care about people (including yourself).
- Forgive someone you really don't want to forgive. Forgiveness is not only a gift to that person, but to yourself. Forgiving doesn't mean that you condone the behavior, just that you're willing to let go of the angry mental dialog you have with that person. Forgiving doesn't mean you even have to like the person, simply that you realize he or she is only human and you let go of judgment.

"Give what you have. To someone, it may be better than you dare think."

Henry Wadsworth Longfellow

Chapter 2

How to deal with stress, guilt, sadness and holiday blues

"You're only here for a short visit. Don't hurry, don't worry. And be sure to smell the flowers along the way."

Walter Hagen, first celebrity golfer

It's not surprising that we feel pressure, depression, frustration and about a dozen other unpleasant emotions during the holiday season. Christmas is meant to be a time of joy, giving, and tradition, a time of celebrating and sharing the love and hope that are the messages of this holiday. And yet in our efforts to make it *special*, we sometimes make it *stressful* by expecting ourselves to *do*, *have* and *be* too much. Then, if our experiences don't live up to our expectations, or we believe they won't, we feel frustrated, sad, maybe guilty, and we suffer from holiday blues.

But this year will be different. One of the keys to enjoying the holidays is to know what you want to feel, and then make sure the things you plan to do will help you achieve your goal. Another key is to do your best and then try not to judge the results.

Take a few minutes to sit down someplace quiet with a blank piece of paper and a pen and ask yourself some questions: *What was Christmas like last year?* Rushed? Nothing special, just another project to complete? Were you frustrated or guilty that you didn't do or feel more? *What would you like to eliminate?* Dinner with Auntie Lindy? Sending cards to people you don't really know anymore? Showing up at seemingly obligatory get-togethers with people from work?

What would you like to have more of? More time with your family and friends? More time to enjoy baking, decorating? More time to think about what the holiday means? More feelings of love, connection and optimism? *What new feelings and experiences would you like to add?* Have you always wanted to go caroling? Would you like to go to a candlelight service? Would you like to feel love for someone it's not easy for you to love? Would you like to forgive someone you haven't been able to forgive?

By having a clear picture of what you want to do and what you want to eliminate, you've got the first tools for eliminating stress and holiday blues. You've probably already figured out that stress occurs when you're out of balance, when two parts of yourself don't agree. For example, one part of you really doesn't want to throw a holiday party and the other part says you have to because others expect it. Or one part of you would like to take the family to a cabin in the woods for Christmas but you know if you did, your parents or other family members would be heartbroken.

I'd like to encourage you to pay more attention to the voice that tells you to do what you *want* to do and less attention to the voice (that you'll usually recognize as someone else's) that says, "Yes, but..." In this chapter are specific ways to eliminate stress, guilt, sadness and blues.

&ۄ &

....

♦ Consider who is most important in your life (hopefully you!) and make your holiday plans with that in mind.

♦ Put off doing whatever you can till January. Don't schedule December appointments with the dentist, paint the living room or buy a new car.

♦ Life is meant to be expressed and enjoyed, not broken down into chores that must be done as quickly as possible and then crossed off the list. Enjoy wrapping gifts—don't just rush to get it done. Enjoy decorating the tree—make it an event rather than an effort.

♦ We'd all like to be Martha Stewart, but most of us aren't. Do what will be fun to do and don't wish it were more. Simple holiday parties and decorations can be the best kind.

♦ The time to recognize you won't have time or energy to do everything you'd like to do is between now and December 25, before you're in the middle of trying.

♦ You were already busy before the season started, so don't expect yourself to do all the holiday shopping, cleaning and cooking yourself. Ask for help. Be specific about what you want and need, and then don't complain about the way it gets done.

♦ Do things according to the 80/20 rule. Do the 20 percent that will make 80 percent of the impact. If you need six dozen cookies for your party at work, make three dozen of two sure-fire hits rather than one dozen each of six. Decorate your house with the high-visibility wreaths, garlands and sprays rather than spending hours hand-stitching beads on a Christmas stocking.

♦ Find ways to play, and don't let that nagging voice convince you that you don't have time.

....

- Do something physical. Go dancing, ice-skating, roller-skating or take a long walk.
- Meditate. It's a perfect excuse to sit and do nothing.

80 QR

Advertisers tell us what we have to do, have, give and be for the holidays because that's their job, not because it's true. Don't let the ads make you feel guilty for not being super human.

Filling every second with *busy-ness* is not efficient, it's *work* and work is stressful. Throw out those books that tell you how to do three things at once and learn to be content to wait at red lights, read something frivolous while waiting for an appointment, or simply sit and do nothing.

We expect so much of ourselves and so little *for* ourselves. Yet it's when we are calm, peaceful and happy that we have the most to give.

Several times a day, take three minutes and simply relax. Breathe deeply, close your eyes and picture a beautiful beach or mountain retreat. Relax your shoulders, jaw, abdomen. What, you don't have three minutes? You need to take six! How comfortable you are with sitting and doing nothing is an indication of how much you need to do it *especially* with the holiday rush. The lower your comfort level, the higher your need.

80 QR

- Try not to get frustrated (and angry) when others don't buy into your must-do list. Don't let them force you to buy into theirs. Stress is relative. Something that you enjoy can be very stressful to another member of your family, and vice versa.
- Avoid, "If you really loved me you'd (fill in the blank)" thoughts.
- Don't let anyone talk you out of the way you feel.

- If you don't want to do something, it's more honest to just say no than to do it grudgingly and hold the other person an emotional hostage.
- Don't take very much personally. Be willing not to insist on being right.
- If it matters what that someone special gives you for a gift, you'd better hint.
- Color-code your December calendar. Ask each family member to mark his or her appointments in a different colored ink pen on a community calendar. It's easier to keep track of people that way.
- Plan an evening with your family to do nothing but enjoy each other. Rent a holiday movie, make decorations, play games or read books.
- Take time to be in awe of the people in your life, of the magic of sunsets and snowflakes and rainbows.

"Our life is frittered away by detail...simplify, simplify."

Henry David Thoreau

In these days of second and third marriages, the numbers of people that can be involved in any family holiday can be staggering. And, in any family, there are still bound to be conflicts about whose family gets you for the special day. Here are some solutions to the whose-family-do-we-celebrate-with dilemma:

- Celebrate with one family Christmas, one on Christmas Eve.
- Celebrate with one family the weekend before Christmas.
- Celebrate with one family this year, the other family next year.
- Invite both families to your house.
- Go away for the holidays.

ℰℴ ℭℛ

Children tend to be creatures of habit, comfortable with routine... and then here come the holidays, full of hype, changed schedules and strangers. Some take it all in their stride and others need special attention to help them adapt. Here are some ways to lower holiday stress with them:

♦ If they act fussy during the holidays, try to treat them at least as well as you like to be treated when you're bored, tired, cranky or anxious.

♦ Practice saying yes instead of no. "Yes, you may have that after you're 21" may seem a bit far off when the child is six, but it's a yes and lots of times it works.

♦ A toddler can usually remember the lessons he or she has learned about eating and being polite. But if the schedule is disrupted during the holidays, behavior regression can occur. Try to maintain the schedule for sleep and meals. Introduce new people gently and let your toddler, not the visitor, determine the allowable level of intimacy.

♦ If a tantrum occurs, remove the child to a remote and quiet place. Demonstrate the calm you want her to exhibit rather than joining her in a tantrum.

♦ Bribe for good behavior before an incident, not to correct bad behavior once it's started. If you're uncomfortable with the concept, you can justify it by telling yourself that most of us go to work because someone bribes us with the promise of a paycheck.

♦ Repeat behavior rules before going into a new situation.

♦ Be consistent. Don't ignore pesky behavior and then explode.

♦ Don't threaten children about Santa. That's stressful to them.

"The surest way to happiness is in losing yourself in a cause greater than yourself."

Solomon (Proverb 10:1)

Every once in awhile ask yourself, "Where am I rushing to get to?" If the answer is that you're rushing to get things done, look for things on that list that you don't really have to do. A good way to help you decide what you *really* have to do and what you only think you have to do is to imagine that someone you care about is in your situation, asking you for advice. What would you suggest?

ℰℬ

Have you ever noticed that if you make a list of 20 things to do and manage to do 18, the two you don't get done are things like meditate or exercise, things you need to do to take care of *you*? During the holidays, such things may not even make it to your list at all! So here are some things to put at the *top*:

♦ Eat well. Pass on 90 percent of the cookies, cakes, candies and celebration drinks that you're offered.

♦ Get enough rest and sleep. Rather than staying up late trying to get everything done, take some of the chores off your "to-do" list.

♦ Exercise.

♦ Meditate. When you're busiest is when it's most important to take that mental health break.

♦ Cut down or eliminate the amount of caffeine in your diet.

♦ Tell people you care about them. You might be surprised how good that makes you feel.

♦ Stop judging (yourself, others and events).

- Let go of strong attachments to the way things turn out. Parties, family celebrations and trips won't always work out the way you'd like them to, but if you aren't locked into the notion that they simply *must,* you won't be as upset when they don't.
- When people offer to help you shop, decorate or clean, let them. If they don't offer, ask them and don't feel guilty. Whoever told you that you had to do it all?
- Bring a small vase to work and keep a flower in your work area every day. Bring in a simple holiday decoration.
- Surround yourself with things that make you happy—books, music, flowers, art.
- Smile at others. Smile at yourself in the mirror.
- Call an old friend to say you miss him or her.
- Give yourself a foot massage daily. On days you go shopping, give yourself two.
- Simplify everything.
- Slow down.

"Laughter is a form of inner jogging."

Norman Cousins

How long have you been promising yourself to slow down? Do you ever wonder why you haven't been successful ? The reason is that you're addicted to that pace, so any time you *don't* have a full schedule, your brain finds other things it tells you you have to do. And your brain will keep on pushing you (with permission from you and urging from others) until you finally say, "Stop!" One way your body says stop is to get sick, then it's not your fault that you have to slow down. You don't have to be sick to slow down. Don't create *dis-ease* to slow down or get out of parties and celebrations you don't want to attend.

ℰℭ

Here are more than twenty ways to slow down this holiday season.

♦ Every day, practice doing a little less than you think you want to or can.

♦ Ask yourself, "What on my list doesn't really have to be done?", "What doesn't have to be done quite so perfectly?" and "What doesn't have to be done by me?", then eliminate and delegate.

♦ Ask about pickup and delivery services for cleaners, drug stores, food markets...a small tip can buy you time to do other things. (Or time to do nothing!)

♦ Do one thing at a time and enjoy doing it. If you're baking Christmas cookies, don't be planning your next shopping trip.

♦ Take time every day to remember at least one reason you love each person you're close to. Stop and *feel* that love.

♦ Realize that you can't do everything. You were already busy before the holidays. Something has to give and sometimes it's your expectations.

♦ Get others to help you. Decide what chores don't have to be done perfectly and ask family members to help you so you have time to do things for them. Agree on when the chores will be done and (here's the hard part), don't remind the chore-doer until the day after the chore was to be done. Train yourself to believe that getting chores done by someone else is better than having them done perfectly by you. Be generous with praise when the chores are done.

♦ Take a break. Go to a movie matinee and see something light. Enjoy a Christmas video and don't answer the phone.

♦ Make time for lazy bubble baths, alone or with someone special. Add candles, soothing music, and float flowers in the water.

♦ Sleep late at least once a week.

♦ There's no law that says you have to answer the phone or the door. When you want to relax, unplug the phone or at least turn off the sound of the bell and message machine.

♦ Get rid of your car phone. You don't need to be accessible every minute.

♦ Practice staying in the moment and try to make it as enjoyable as possible. Often, all it takes is a mind shift. While stuck in traffic, you can curse the traffic or be thankful you have a car or money for other transportation.

♦ Allow extra time to get to appointments. Rushing is stressful.

♦ Let your spouse shop for gifts for his or her own relatives.

♦ Mass-produced holiday letters might not be acceptable to Miss Manners, but your family and friends will agree they're better than no letters at all.

♦ Take time to ponder possibilities.

♦ When you've got too much on your mind, write it down. Keep a journal, make a list. Stop that mind chatter from chasing itself around in your head by getting it onto paper.

♦ Quit going to group meetings you don't look forward to. If you need an excuse, blame the added activities during the holidays. If you find you miss the people or the activities you can always go back in January.

♦ Make friends with your higher power and get together regularly.

♦ Be patient with yourself if you're trying to change. Remember, change is a process, not an event.

"The best and most beautiful things in the world cannot be seen or even touched. They must be felt with the heart."

Helen Keller

Company's coming *when?* Grab a clean pillowcase, pick up everything on the floor and put it in the pillowcase. Hide the pillowcase in the closet. Assign everyone who's home a different room to tidy. If you run out of pillowcases, use grocery bags.

❊ ❊ ❊

Have instant snacks on hand for these surprise visits: smoked nuts, special candies, chips, pretzels, gouda cheese.

❊ ❊ ❊

If you're uncomfortable with the question, "What did you get for Christmas?" or "Did Santa bring you everything you wanted?" just smile, say, "Everything" or "Yes" and change the subject.

❊ ❊ ❊

Don't hang around with people who are caught up in worry, hurry, anger, disappointment or fear.

❊ ❊ ❊

Unless you love challenges, don't buy anything that says, "Some assembly required."

❊ ❊ ❊

Guilt is the reaction to the old messages of other people who wanted you to do what they wanted you to do and convinced you that if you didn't, you weren't very nice, considerate, responsible or (fill in the blank). Guilty feelings can run rampant during the holidays.

When instilled by our parents, guilt was meant to be a helpful thing. Helpful to them because it gave them an excellent way to control us and helpful to us because it was supposed to let us know the difference between right and wrong.

By the time we're adults, guilt still signals the separation between what we want to do and what we think we should do. The difference is that now it's okay for us to do what we want to do and the "should" messages aren't necessarily true.

Here are some thoughts that can help you avoid holiday guilt trips:

♦ Guilt is a habit. To break it, you have to stop letting yourself indulge in it.

♦ The stronger you believe that you deserve to determine your own life, the less power guilt—the messages of others who want to control your life—will be.

♦ Repeat after me: "It's not my job to make everybody happy."

♦ Eliminate the words "should" and "shouldn't" from your vocabulary.

♦ *"No" is a Complete Sentence: Learning the Sacredness of Personal Boundaries,* by Megan LeBoutillier offers support if you have trouble saying no and sticking to it. The paperback edition is $5.99—a good gift to yourself.

♦ Often when you try to listen to your heart, your head will shout all the reasons why you shouldn't. Thank your head for being concerned and follow your heart.

♦ Generally, your family would rather have fewer decorations, fewer fancy dinners and a happy, relaxed, patient and available you. Don't feel guilty if you can't do it all.

80 Q3

One of the greatest stress-reducers in the world is letting go of attachments to outcomes. Try not to have a mental script of how people "should" act and what they should say or do. If your family has different ideas about how to celebrate the holidays, don't feel betrayed. Try to be happy with your accomplishments whether or not everything turns out perfectly.

Letting go of attachments does *not* mean you don't care what gifts you buy or receive or how your party turns out. It's important to have preferences, plans and goals, but the difference between attachments and goals is how you feel when something doesn't happen the way you want it to. If you feel anger, frustration, resentment, jealousy, victimization, guilt, stress or other unpleasant sensations, you're attached to an outcome.

There are hundreds of opportunities to practice letting go of attachments to outcomes during the holidays. Whenever you notice an unpleasant feeling, think about what attachment caused it. Then ask yourself if you can let go of having to control the outcome. The more attachments you can let go of, the more you will be able to eliminate stress, guilt, sadness and blues. Please, don't be critical of yourself if you forget or have a hard time making the shift. Don't even be attached to letting go of attachments!

ಏ ಅ
....

Learning to let go of judgments is another stress-reducer and is another message of Christmas that benefits both the giver and receiver.

Notice how your body feels whenever you have a negative judgment. Tense, tight—maybe you feel it as a headache, neck ache, backache, or stomachache. The stronger the judgment, the stronger the feeling.

Letting go of judgments has just three steps: deciding to, noticing when you have one and asking yourself what it would be like if you let it go. The result will be a calmer, happier, less-stressed you.

❊ ❊ ❊

Don't put up with something that causes you stress. If your pen leaks ink all over your greeting cards, get a new pen. If your alarm clock isn't reliable, replace it. If your filing system leaves you always searching and never finding, take some time to develop a new system.

❊ ❊ ❊

Mail gifts early. This eliminates the stress of standing in long lines at the post office or paying a hefty fee to send them by special mail.

❊ ❊ ❊

It's okay to send Christmas cards after the holidays. It's also okay not to send them at all.

....

✳ ✳ ✳

Develop a peaceful place you can go in your mind—the beach, a beautiful mountain clearing—and go there often. Smell the smells. Hear the sounds. Feel the sun, wind or rain on your skin. Imagine the perfect Christmas tree and enjoy decorating it.

ℰℭ

Whoever said, "You can't go home," was wrong. You *can* go home. The trouble is that if you have fond memories of that home, it will have changed and if you have *unpleasant* memories, it won't have. The people you're going home to visit are pretty much the same people they were the last time you saw them. So if you had a good time last year, chances are you'll have a good time this year. If you didn't, you probably won't.

Still, there are tricks to doing anything comfortably and most of them are about attitudes. So here are some thoughts to take with you that will help you maintain your holiday spirit:

- ♦ Forget about winning discussions with family members. If you couldn't before, you can't now. Find things to love about these people and hold onto those thoughts instead.

- ♦ Write down 10 things your family will ask that make you crazy and figure out a response now.

- ♦ Read the paper before you go so you can have a selection of subjects to launch into if you don't like where the current one's going. Look for topics that appeal to your sense of humor.

- ♦ Avoid the temptation to parent your parents.

- ♦ If you want to be right all the time so your family will recognize how smart you are, guess what? So do they.

- ♦ Ask yourself what lesson you can learn by being with these people and then ask yourself what you have to do to learn it.

♦ Don't just be a guest. Your parents took care of you for a long time and might enjoy your willingness to take care of them sometimes. Don't take it personally if they refuse your help, though.

♦ Don't interpret tones of voices, nuances of words, facial expressions or body language. Don't take anything your family members say or do personally, even if you're sure they meant you to.

♦ Don't expect them to finally realize what a hardworking, responsible, loving (fill in the blank) person you are if they didn't realize it on your last visit. It's what *you* know about yourself that's important.

♦ Hear the love behind the message instead of the words. Of *course* you're old enough to know it's cold outside and you'd better "bundle up," but maybe they can't come right out and say, "I love you." Or maybe they can, but they want to say it again this way.

♦ Speak up early when a subject's off limits. Don't wait till you want to strangle them. You might even remind them about off-limit topics while you're planning the visit.

♦ Look for win/win solutions to conflicts.

♦ Ask a friend to call you with support while you're there if you think you're going to need it.

♦ If your teen balks at holiday get-togethers, ask her what she dreads most and then together, figure out ways to make it less terrible. Calling Grandma and asking her not to grill your daughter about boyfriends could be one of those ways.

♦ Keep your sense of humor. Try to find things to laugh about rather than things to feel bad about.

♦ If you're visiting in-laws, don't be fragile. Don't take anything personally, and don't keep score. Show them all the best reasons your spouse chose you. Don't do it for your spouse or your in-laws though, do it for you.

℘ ♋

....

The flip side of going home for the holidays is being the home others *come* to. It's not likely that you'll escape without some potentials for stress. Here are some ways to eliminate most of it, though:

♦ Try to treat your children like grownups. Messages that scold, disapprove or warn make them feel like you don't recognize their competency.

♦ Expect them to follow your house rules while they're there.

♦ Focus on things you have in common rather than ways you're different.

♦ Be a good role model and try not to brag about what a good role model you are.

℘ ♋

....

Years of parental training have convinced us that the holidays are "supposed" to be celebrated joyously with family members, but it can be expensive to arrange for holiday visits, tiring to drive hours and not get to sleep in your own bed, frustrating that a holiday you sacrificed so much for didn't turn out to be the loving experience you expected. And maybe you just want to celebrate some other way this year.

If you decide not to go home, prepare yourself for all the possible responses designed to make you feel guilty, ungrateful, unappreciative, heartless, cold—whatever your family's specialties are—and prepare your responses in advance. Write them down and keep the notes near the phone. When the guilt trips start, don't get carried away by them. Look for ways to help them accept your decisions but don't be at-tached to your wish to make them accept it graciously.

♦ Reassure them that you love them but are unable to come home because you have other plans.

♦ Give as few facts about those plans as possible.

♦ Suggest an alternate time for a visit if you want to.

....

♦ Understand they're disappointed and let them have their feelings.

♦ Resist giving in to guilt. Guilt expands to fill the space you'll let it occupy.

♦ Remember, you're not an awful person just because you want to determine the events in your own life.

♦ Don't let them talk you into changing your plans.

T.S. Eliot said that tradition "cannot be inherited, and if you want it you must obtain it by great labor." Perhaps part of that labor is remaining firm in your desire to create your own traditions.

✳ ✳ ✳

If your holiday plans include driving, look for ways to make the trip a celebration, rather than just a means to get someplace.

♦ Check your tires, oil, transmission fluid, battery and heater a couple of weeks before you go. Pack survival gear (warm coats, sturdy walking shoes, flashlights, water) just in case.

♦ Bring along tapes of Christmas carols. Take gifts you've already received of candy, nuts and fruitcakes to snack on.

♦ Plan to take an extra day or two if you can so you can stop at interesting places along the way.

♦ If you're traveling with kids, try to stop for short breaks. Bring along their skates—a good way to work off energy. Bring along car games and toys, a personal cassette player and tapes.

℘ ℘

Messages about the holidays being a time for family and togetherness can be painful if you have to work on Christmas or if you're traveling and find yourself miles away from home. Or perhaps you'll be home, but your family lives too far away to visit or they will be working or traveling. Don't just accept that you'll have a lonely holiday, plan ways to make it special.

- ♦ Initiate a potluck dinner, invite everyone you know and ask them to bring friends.
- ♦ Take a short trip, even a day trip, to some place you've always wanted to visit but never have.
- ♦ Take a short trip to a place you've already been and enjoyed.
- ♦ Have a picnic by yourself at home. Surround yourself with good food, good music and good books.
- ♦ Take a long walk and count your blessings.
- ♦ Check with your local churches. Most have singles groups that have potluck dinners on Thanksgiving, Christmas and New Year's Day. They welcome strangers. Many have another event early in January to help relieve after-the-holiday blues.
- ♦ Indulge yourself in a long phone call to someone you care about. Plan ahead so you know they'll be home.
- ♦ Look for ways to share what you have with others.
- ♦ If you're scheduled to work, plan a special dinner with others on your shift. Have someone bring a carved turkey, someone else bring a salad, cranberry sauce, pie, etc. If you work with children, as do flight personnel and medical staff, bring holiday candies to share. Play Christmas music, sing along and during breaks, share stories of favorite holidays in the past.
- ♦ If you're out of town on business during the holidays, get together with others from your company who are away from home. Accept invitations of locals when they invite you to share the holidays with them. Treat yourself to a wonderful dinner, a special concert or play. Be a tourist and check out the city's special attractions.

၅၁ ၉၃
....

Moving is almost always stressful, no matter how much you've planned for it. Moving near the holidays may be even more stressful if you have holiday traditions that include people and events in your old home town. Here are some ways you can help yourself feel more comfortable:

- Play music you enjoyed in your previous home.
- Go to the same kinds of places you enjoyed in your old neighborhood: churches, bookstores, coffee houses, health food stores, libraries. Sign up for classes—art, yoga, meditation, cooking, wine tasting, language, dance.
- Call trusted friends to talk. It's worth the long-distance charges if it makes you feel better.
- Let people know you're new in town. Ask them about their favorite things to do for the holidays.
- Read the local paper and decide to do at least one fun thing every week.
- Dress up your new home with all your old favorite holiday decorations.
- When your kids say they're lonely or unhappy, avoid the temptation to try to make them feel better by discounting their feelings or making them look at the "bright" side. Psychologists are telling us how important it is to feel our feelings rather than deny them. It's tough to be a parent and see your children be unhappy, but the best response is often just to say, "I know" or maybe, "I know, I feel that way sometimes, too."

၅၁ ၉၃
....

Unfortunately, there are always some people who don't share the holiday spirit, and in fact they prey on people who are too trusting. Unless you live in a particularly dangerous area, there's no reason to be paranoid, but it's smart to be aware of possible dangers and take precautions.

- ◆ Don't leave packages visible in your car.
- ◆ Be skeptical of people selling "gold" jewelry on the streets.
- ◆ Be skeptical of telephone calls for charities you've never heard of or from callers you suspect are not legitimate.
- ◆ Be aware that tickets to holiday shows that are sold on the street may be counterfeit.

＊ ＊ ＊

There are also some "natural" disasters to avoid. Here are some thoughts to tuck in the back of your mind.

- ◆ Examine tree light wires for frays and discard any that are questionable.
- ◆ Don't burn real candles on trees.
- ◆ For outdoor lights, only use lights that are labeled for outdoor use.
- ◆ Don't discard your Christmas tree in the fireplace.
- ◆ Don't set up your tree near fireplaces or radiators.
- ◆ Don't burn colored paper in the fireplace, as the fumes can be toxic.
- ◆ Avoid party foods that would normally be refrigerated and have been on a buffet table for hours.
- ◆ Be aware of holly berries, mistletoe, Jerusalem cherry, amaryllis and other plants that can cause severe stomach problems to children and pets if eaten.

৪৩ ೕ

More people get the blues during the holidays than any other time of the year, and it's easy to see why. It's the time when our expectations are highest. We're exposed to some very fancy and very expensive goodies and told we deserve it. It's true, we tell ourselves, we *do* deserve it. And that may make us sad because we know we can't have it, perhaps never will have it. We forget that most of the other people on this planet deserve it and they won't have it either.

We read about people who epitomize the gracious host and hostess and we know that we could be just as gracious if we had their money, their maids, their nannies. But we don't and wonder how we failed.

We see glimpses of happy, loving families and maybe ours isn't quite that happy or loving, or maybe we're alone. Or we *do* have a happy loving, family and we want to buy them wonderful gifts to show them how much we love them, but the MasterCard is tapped out from when the water heater exploded.

The opportunities for the blues are endless, but so are the remedies:

- Find something nice to do for yourself every day. Listen to your favorite Christmas music, buy a bunch of flowers, burn incense, take a long bubble bath.

- Release your expectations about feelings and events and just enjoy whatever good comes along.

- Focus on understanding rather than being understood, on loving rather being loved.

- Plan something to do after all the presents are opened. Rent a fun movie, play board games, serve the holiday meal. Go out and admire local lights or the decorations in a fancy hotel. Look for ways to keep the feeling of connectedness to people or to your higher power.

- Find an older person and invite him or her to share fond holiday memories.

- Stop and listen to the rain, watch the snow or walk in the sun.

- Find opportunities to hug. It'll make you feel great. If there's no one to hug, hug a tree. Honest—it works!

- Look for reasons to giggle.

ℬ ℭ

Sometimes we get so caught up in the role of parenting that it's easy to overlook some of the lessons we can learn from children.

- They ask for what they want and need.
- They trust.
- They forgive and forget.
- They enjoy themselves completely in the moment.
- They feel their feelings.
- They laugh joyously.
- They don't judge the gift by its price tag.
- They love wholeheartedly.
- They ask for food when they're hungry, drink when they're thirsty, and they sleep when they're tired.
- They don't judge themselves or other people (until they're taught to).

"Life is too important to be taken seriously."

Oscar Wilde

Slow down. Simplify. Be childlike.

Sing in the shower. Dance in the rain.

Chapter 3

Hassle-free celebrations and entertaining

"I always prefer to believe the best of everybody — it saves so much trouble."

Rudyard Kipling

Does it seem like the words "hassle-free" and "celebrations" don't belong in the same sentence? Do you try to go to all the holiday parties, host some yourself and spare no expense of time or money on decorations and food? Or do you ignore the festivities completely to avoid the hassle?

This year you can find a happy place somewhere in the middle. It's easy to enjoy your celebrations. The key is to plan what you want to do early in the season.

Start thinking early in December about what you want to celebrate and how. Let everyone in the family make suggestions and get promises of help now so you don't end up doing all the work yourself.

Try to avoid filling up your social calendar with busy events and, instead, look for ways to celebrate that capture the spirit of the holidays. Look for ways that bring you closer to people you care about and lead to traditions you can enjoy year after year.

- Buy or make an ornament every year. If you make it, let it reflect something special that happened during the year. If you buy one, select one that fills you with joy.
- Choose a date, like December 1, and decorate your home on that date every year. Make decorating a family event.
- Buy an advent calendar—one for you and one for the kids—and enjoy lifting the window every day to see what's hidden underneath.
- Draw family names. Be that person's Santa or Guardian Angel all through the month. Don't tell who got whose name.
- Draw names in your family and every day write a short note to that person with reasons you're thankful for him or her. Draw a new name each week.

During December, have a family night once a week. Use this time to talk about family goals, values and express love and appreciation for each other. If schedules don't permit getting together, let everyone tack their thoughts on a bulletin board or use sticky notes and put them on the refrigerator.

"There are two ways to live your life. One is as though nothing is a miracle. The other is as though everything is a miracle."

Albert Einstein

As an alternative to hosting a party, arrange a house-to-house or progressive party. Let one couple host appetizers at their house, the next host soup and salads, the next a main course and the last serves dessert.

❋ ❋ ❋

Get together with some of your closest friends and have an ornament swap party. If you're brave, make the ornaments by hand.

෩ ଔ

Read a book out loud every night in December to your children. If you don't want to buy dozens of books, check them out at your public library. Here are some of my Christmas favorites:

- ◆ *A Christmas Guest*, David LaRochelle. A young boy remembers an earlier Christmas Eve and the surprising result of his generosity.
- ◆ *The Angel Academy*, Misty Taggart. Ten fun stories that communicate values to children as five mischievous guardian angels in training work to earn their wings.
- ◆ *The Nativity Play*, Nick Butterworth and Mick Inkpen. The nativity is explained in this fun book as children present the story as a play.
- ◆ *The Perfect Christmas Gift*, Judy Delton. Bear has a hard time finding the perfect gift for Duck and discovers that friendship is really the best gift. For young readers.
- ◆ *Danny and the Three Kings*, Susan Cooper. Because his mother can't afford a tree, Danny tries to get one for his baby brother. This has frustrating and then surprising results.
- ◆ *Merry Christmas With Love*, Sandi Patti. A story about how two neighbors discover the greatest Christmas gift of all.
- ◆ *Santa Calls*, William Joyce. An exquisite alphabet pop-up book.
- ◆ *A Christmas Alphabet*, Robert Sabuda. A popular alphabet book for very young children.

ဆ ભ

Hanukkah usually falls in December, too, and here are some fun books about this celebration:

♦ *The Chanukah Guest,* Eric A. Kimmel. Bubba (Grandmother) Brayna prepares a wonderful Chanukah celebration for the Rabbi. But Bubba doesn't see very well so when Old Bear comes to visit, she welcomes him, thinking it's the Rabbi. When Old Bear is full of food and rested from eating so much, he ambles off. Imagine Bubba's surprise when the Rabbi arrives a little later!

♦ *The Hanukkah Book,* Marilyn Burns. Recipes, crafts, gifts, games, songs and a chapter about the experience of Christmas for Jewish families are included in this book for older children.

♦ *The Power of Light: Eight Stories for Hanukkah,* Isaac Basheivis Singer. For young children.

♦ *All About Hanukkah,* Judye Groner and Madeline Wilker. This tells the story of Hanukkah and talks about the holiday today, candle lighting and blessing, the dreidel and the freedom to be different.

ဆ ભ

Kwanzaa is an African-American celebration that begins on December 26 and lasts for eight days. Two books about Kwanzaa are:

♦ *Let's Celebrate Kwanzaa: An Activity Book for Young Readers,* Helen Davis Thompson. This book describes the seven principles of the holiday and suggests fun activities that help kids think about what the principles mean in their lives.

♦ *The Story of Kwanzaa,* Safisha L. Madhubuti. There is some very basic history of Africans in Africa and how the seven principles were part of their lives.

---

*Not everyone celebrates Christmas, but
everyone is included in the greeting,
"Happy Holidays."*

Holiday traditions don't have to be major events; actually, they can be quite simple. Notice things you do that you really enjoy and turn them into traditions. For example:

♦ Each year, spend one evening making ornaments.
♦ If you open gifts on Christmas day, exchange one or two small gifts on Christmas Eve. Include guests if you have them.
♦ If you and your spouse open gifts in a crowd, find a special time when you can be alone to exchange a special gift.
♦ Save at least one thing to celebrate on the day after Christmas. It might be fun to exchange simple handmade gifts or cards with your family.

ℰ ℭ

If you remember the days when you used to make 27 different kinds of cookies from scratch and wish you still had the time, here's the next best thing: Have a homemade cookie swap party. Here's how:

♦ Pick an early date to swap. The date should be about two weeks before Christmas.
♦ Get a firm commitment from those who agree to come.
♦ Ask each to tell you what he or she plans to bring so you can avoid duplication.
♦ Each should bring several selections, in bags of at least half a dozen, plus a few for sampling.
♦ Ask each guest to attach the recipe to each bag of cookies.
♦ Have snacks to serve at the party.

ℰℭ ℭℛ

Let go of traditions that have outlived their purpose. If you dread an event, stop going. You may feel that you're letting others down if you don't go, but you'll be letting yourself down if you go. You'll be angry and feel like a victim of emotional blackmail. Here are five honest excuses you can give:

♦ *"I have been looking forward to starting some of my own traditions and I won't be able to come to your event this year."* Don't elaborate on your new tradition. If asked, say, "You know, I'd really like to tell you about it afterward." Don't justify your position and don't give in.

♦ *"I'm going to be away that day."* Be vague about where if it's not someplace far away.

♦ *"I'd love to see you, but that day isn't going to work out. What about lunch on (pick a date)?"*

♦ *"I won't be able to stay, but I'd like to drop in for a minute to say hello."*

♦ *"I'm going to spend the whole day pretty much alone (be vague), but I'll be there with you in thought."*

Remember, you have every right to choose how to spend your time and everything others say will be said to try to get you to change your mind. Guilt comes in many forms, but all of them are spelled c-o-n-t-r-o-l.

"Each day, and the living of it, has to be a conscious creation in which discipline and order are relieved with some play and pure foolishness."

May Sarton, American writer

ℰℭ

....

One of the reasons entertaining is stressful is because there are some things we forget about altogether and other things we think so much about we end up creating a "to-do" list that would take a staff of six to complete. Here are some ideas to help you make entertaining simpler:

♦ If you're having a party and guests will be bringing young children, hire a babysitter to keep them entertained in another room.

♦ Hire babysitters early.

♦ Don't offer to have a big dinner at your house unless you really enjoy cooking for lots of people.

♦ If you hire a caterer, ask what will be included. Beverages? A server? It's better to ask too many questions than not enough.

♦ Consider serving only white wine at your home parties. If red wine is spilled it can ruin carpets and upholstery and it would make both you and the spiller feel awful.

♦ Be understanding when someone you'd like to have join you at a celebration says no—no matter what the reason.

ℰℭ

....

Give up your fantasies about children behaving perfectly during a holiday dinner. Murphy's Law applies in any setting with children and high expectations. Children will act like children no matter how much you wish they would act like little adults.

Coach children before a party or a big family gathering. Most children are natural hams and you may be able to appeal to their thespian nature if you rehearse them in greeting strangers, being polite and enduring hugs from enthusiastic relatives. Then again, you may not.

Children may misbehave during social events, believing that you won't correct them, but if you ignore bad behavior, it will escalate. Try removing them to a soundproofed room, or at least one as far from the festivities as possible, and explain the rules again.

Review rules before you bring your children into a social setting. They can be the same rules you use during the year when you go out to dinner: no running, no screaming, no banging things on the table or floor—or whatever reminders are important for your young ones.

> *"Of course I don't always enjoy being a mother. At those times my husband and I hole up somewhere in the wine country, eat, drink, make mad love and pretend we were born sterile and raise poodles."*
>
> *Dorothy DeBolt, recipient of the 1980 National Mother's Day Committee Award*

First holidays after a divorce can be hard for you—and they can be especially hard on children. This may be a good time to begin some new traditions. Consider changing the usual meal to one that the kids like. All pitch in to cook, or order pizza. Get together to decide on some other traditions you'd all enjoy, maybe a ride through the neighborhood with the most Christmas decorations, or maybe going to a movie. Talk to your children, though, and find out which traditions they don't want to give up. They might want and need the security of some of the same activities.

Encourage the kids to talk about how they feel and don't try to talk them out of feeling badly. Much as it hurts to see them unhappy, the feelings have to be felt before they will go away.

Suggest they make the other parent a special gift or a card. If they expect something from the other parent (and they should expect *something*), it might be a good idea to gently coach your ex about gifts the children might like. Try to avoid demands or language that says you think he or she couldn't have thought of great ideas alone.

ΩΩ CR

If you feel like you gain weight just *thinking* about food, the holidays can definitely be hazardous to your health. But there are ways to cut down on the calories:

◆ Eat an apple, banana, yogurt or a piece of bread to curb your appetite before you go to a celebration.

◆ At a buffet, take the small plate. Take small servings and limit yourself to three or four choices. Eat slowly. Wait 10 minutes after finishing before you go back. *Try* not to go back.

◆ Avoid foods with cheese or sauces.

◆ Choose white turkey/chicken without skin.

◆ If you have dessert, choose pumpkin pie rather than pecan. Choose pies without whipped cream or ice cream.

◆ Discourage food and drink pushers by leaving some food on your plate and drink in your glass.

◆ Take some sugar-free hard candies to (discreetly) suck on.

◆ Avoid snacks that are salty or spicy—they'll encourage more drinking.

◆ Avoid anything you can eat by the handfuls.

◆ Ask for low-cal beverages.

◆ Don't stand by the buffet table.

◆ Focus on socializing, not eating.

◆ In restaurants, ask to have your meat broiled or baked rather than fried. Request salad dressings and sauces on the side. Eat half and take the rest home for lunch. Have soup or salad and split the main course with someone else.

◆ If you're hosting the party, include low-fat or nonfat and vegetarian dishes. Replace eggnog with hot spiced tea. Before the party, store tempting snack food where you won't see it.

ဢ ✆

It's possible to survive two dinners on one day if you eat small portions. Have only appetizers and soup or salad at one place and the main course at the other.

ဢ ✆

Another way to cut down on holiday calories is to have parties that don't focus on food—for example, a caroling party. Here are some tips to help you host one:

- Choose a date as soon as possible.
- Plan where you're going. If there's a convalescent home or hospital nearby, see if they'd like you to visit.
- Ask guests to bring candles, flashlights and an empty thermos.
- Provide copies of typed words to popular carols.
- Serve low-cal finger foods while waiting for everyone to arrive.
- Fill thermoses with hot chocolate, coffee or spiced cider to take with you.
- Serve warm food—chili or soup—after caroling.

ဢ ✆

People moan and groan about playing party games. But the truth is, they have a great time if the game is fun. The key is in selecting the right game. Here's a simple mixer: Before the party, make up a list of things your guests might have done. The number you come up with should be more than the number of guests you have. Since the idea is for people to meet, it's better to have too many possibilities than too few. Type them up on a list, include a space for a name after each item and make more than enough copies for everyone.

For example, some of the items on the list might be: Stayed up all night to watch the sun rise; visited an island within the last three years; is an only child, speaks another language fluently. When coming up with ideas, keep your guests in mind. With some crowds, the list could be much more lively.

When a good number of guests are there, pass out the sheets and let people find someone who fits each category. (Each person can only fit one category.) Since the goal is for people to meet, announce that there's no rush, the game will continue for 30 minutes.

❊ ❊ ❊

Here's another fun game (trust me): Ask guests to bring a wrapped "white elephant" (a fun item that you own but don't use anymore). Each guest draws a number, and the person with the lowest number goes first. He or she selects a wrapped gift, opens it and the person with the next-lowest number has the choice of taking that gift or taking a wrapped gift. If the second player takes the first player's gift, the first person gets to choose again. Then it's the third player's turn. Each gift can only be "stolen" three times, then it stays where it is.

Another variation, and more fun with the right crowd, is that the first player chooses a wrapped package and opens it. If the next player wants it, he or she must argue why he or she deserves it more, and then the first player must argue his or her deservedness. The group decides who is more convincing, the losing player chooses another wrapped gift and the play continues.

80 CR

....

If you want some holiday music but are stumped about what to choose, try these top-selling Christmas albums (according to *Billboard*): *Miracles: The Holiday Album* by Kenny G and *Merry Christmas* by Mariah Carey.

ℰℭ

The libraries are full of good books on decorating and recipes for celebrations. *My First Christmas Activity Book: A Step-by-step Guide to Making Fun Things for Christmas* by Angela Wilkes, is okay for older children and great for adults. It shows how to make advent calendars, gift wrapping, cards, festive cookies, candies, wreaths, potpourri, tree decorations and more.

Here are nearly a dozen simple decorations you can make with your family:

- Make a garland by starting with a length of rope. Use florist wire to attach bunches of holly or pine sprays and small pine cones. Twist greenery around the rope so the rope doesn't show, and anchor it with the florist wire.
- Hang Christmas cards on your tree.
- String gummy bears or gummy fish and Jujubes with dental floss for tree ornaments or garlands.
- Tie raffia or fabric ribbon bows to tree branches.
- Tie cinnamon sticks with a bow and hang them on the tree.
- Cut decorations out of cardboard. Punch a hole at the top and decorate with glossy paint.
- Cut decorations out of washed Styrofoam meat trays, dip them in glue and then glitter. Punch a hole at the top and tie with ribbon or yarn.
- Cut paper snowflakes. Fold paper and cut, just like you did when you were a kid.
- Wrap your front door and your mailbox like presents.
- Put a wreath on the front of your car or fasten a little tree to the radio antennae.

ℰℴ ℭℛ

Another project not so simple but fun, is making pretzel decorations.

1 pkg. yeast
1½ cup warm water
1 tbs. sugar
1 tbs. salt
4 cups flour
1 egg
coarse salt

Combine yeast, water, sugar and salt in a large bowl. Stir in flour and knead on a flat surface until the dough is smooth. Take a small amount of dough at a time, roll it so it's long and slender, then bend it into letters or shapes. Add small amounts of flour as needed to keep dough from sticking to your hands. Put on a greased cookie sheet, brush with beaten egg, sprinkle lightly with salt before baking or dip in salt immediately after removing from the oven. Bake in preheated oven, 425 degrees for 15 minutes or until golden.

You can hang your pretzel creations on the tree as decorations or tie them to gift packages.

ℰℴ ℭℛ

Luminarias are a tradition of the Southwest (like strings of chili pepper lights) that are catching on across the country. Generally, they're used outdoors to light a walkway or decorate a porch. There are different ways you can make luminarias. Here are two:

To make punched tin luminarias, wash and remove the paper from a tin can, mark a pattern for holes with a magic marker, freeze water in the can to help it hold its shape and then use an ice pick on the marked spots. Let the ice melt and burn a votive candle inside. If you use these inside, leave enough room below the holes to hold all the melted wax. When lit, be sure you've put something under the can in case it gets hot or leaks.

Another way to make luminarias is to punch holes in white bakery bags or brown lunch bags. Put sand, gravel, course salt or kitty litter in the bottom of the bag and press a votive candle (in a glass holder for greatest safety) into the material at the bottom of the bag.

ഐ ca
....

If you like to cook and bake, you probably have hundreds of wonderful recipes to dazzle your friends with, and every holiday you add a hundred more. If you don't like to cook, I have some recipes from my more domestic days. They're *simple*, but show-stoppers.

Mexican Pralines

1 cup firmly packed brown sugar
1 cup granulated sugar
1 T. corn syrup
1 T. butter or margarine
5 T. water
2 cups whole pecans or walnuts

Heat the first five ingredients in saucepan to 230 degrees, add nuts, drop on waxed paper. That's it.

Fantastic Ice Cream Pie

15 oz. of crushed chocolate sandwich cookies
1 cube margarine, melted
½ gal. coffee ice cream
1 large tub of whipped topping
small package slivered almonds
1 16-oz can fudge sauce

Mash cookies, add melted butter. Press onto the bottom of two pie plates or one sheet cake pan. Freeze 20 to 30 minutes. Add ice cream, freeze. Cover with fudge sauce, freeze. Cover with whipped topping and almonds, freeze. Cover and store until serving time.

Remove from the freezer five minutes before serving. Note: It's easier to cut if you can remove it from the pan, so if your guests won't see this until it appears on their plates, line the pan with foil, leaving flaps over the sides, and the lift the whole thing to a flat surface to cut.

Dazzling Chocolate Cake

Make your favorite box-mix chocolate cake and a double recipe of chocolate buttercream frosting. When the cake is cool, invert one layer onto a serving plate and use frosting to build a 1-inch rim (like a wall) on top of the cake around the edge. Fill the resulting well with 1 can cherry pie filling (add a tablespoon of rum extract, if you want to). Carefully place the second layer on and frost as usual. Decorate with maraschino cherries and shaved chocolate.

Easy Buñuelos

¼ cup sugar
¼ t. cinnamon
4 small flour tortillas
vegetable oil

Mix sugar and cinnamon, use scissors or a pizza cutter to cut each tortilla into four wedges. Heat oil. Drop tortilla wedges in hot oil a few at a time. Cook until golden brown, remove to absorbent paper towels and immediately sprinkle with sugar/cinnamon mixture. Repeat process until all are done. Serve immediately. Variation: Instead of granulated sugar and cinnamon, sprinkle with powdered sugar.

Greg Baker's Sautéed Strawberries

Slice strawberries and sauté in butter. Add 1-drink-size bottle Grand Marnier. Serve alone or over ice cream.

Stuffed Dates

1 box pitted dates
1 cup almonds
powdered sugar

Stuff an almond into each date, roll it in a small bowl of powdered sugar. Store covered.

ℰℭ

Here are some delicious cookies kids can make:

Russian Tea Cakes (Mexican Wedding Cakes)

2 sticks softened margarine
½ cup sifted powdered sugar
1 t. vanilla
2¼ cups sifted flour
¼ t. salt
¾ cup walnuts chopped fine

Combine all ingredients and chill dough. Roll in 1-inch balls and place on ungreased baking sheet. Bake until set but not brown. Roll in powdered sugar while still warm. Bake at 400 degrees 10 to 12 minutes, until done but not brown. Makes about four dozen cookies.

Healthy Ones/Peanut Butter Carob Balls

½ cup carob powder
½ cup honey
½ cup natural peanut butter (room temp.)
½ cup sunflower seeds
½ cup sesame seeds
½ cup uncooked oatmeal
shredded coconut to taste

Combine everything in a large bowl, blend by hand. When blended, form into 1-inch balls. Do not cook! Store in plastic container in the refrigerator.

> *"Do not let trifles disturb your tranquility of mind...Life is too precious to be sacrificed for the nonessential and transient... Ignore the inconsequential."*
>
> *Grenville Kleiser*

Pets are part of the family, but we may forget about them when we plan for the holidays. Some pets seem complacent no matter what goes on, but others can be confused or disturbed by crowds of people or a change in routine. So here are some ways to be good to your pets:

♦ Make a place available for your pet to get away from the crowd.

♦ Don't show off your pet if he'd rather be by himself.

♦ Try to keep your pet on a regular schedule of feeding, grooming and walking.

♦ Keep holiday decorations and tree light cords above your pet's reach.

&() ()&

Holiday festivities can be hazardous to your financial health, but there are lots of ways to celebrate with the family that are well within anyone's budget. Here are a few ideas:

♦ Enjoy doing nothing with your family. Build a fire in the fireplace, munch on popcorn or cookies...encourage others to tell you something good that happened to them during the week.

♦ Don't save your best dishes and glasses for company—use them for your *own* enjoyment.

♦ Visit the lobby of great hotels to see their decorations.

♦ Have a candlelight dinner even if it's just you and the kids.

♦ Buy a couple of big fat candles and light them often.

♦ Drive slowly past the town's nicest decorations. Take along a thermos of hot chocolate.

♦ Have a potluck with friends and neighbors who may not have family nearby.

♦ Go to a candlelight church service.

☙ ❧
....

It's disappointing when your holiday photographs don't turn out, and the fact is that even with today's "aim-and-shoot" cameras, it's possible to take some really bad pictures. When you're ready to shoot a special moment is not the time to discover your camera or flash battery are dead. To be safe, replace them both and buy extra film the first week of December.

Before you push the button to commit the image to film, scan the outer edges of the viewfinder to make sure you aren't cutting off your subject's body in awkward places: at the ankles, knees, hips and lower chest. Notice the background so you don't have trees or poles coming out of your subject's head.

☙ ❧
....

There are some pretty good reasons not to buy a real Christmas tree this year—the expense is one and the landfill shortage is another. Americans cut down more than 35 million Christmas trees a year. Many are grown for that reason so they're not all taken from the forest—but imagine the space it takes to hold them after the holidays!

There are some fun alternatives, though, and one is to get an artificial tree. The better ones are even nicer looking than the real thing and they stay fresh forever. Other options are to buy a live tree and plant it after the holidays or decorate the houseplants you already have. If you do use a disposable tree, call your city's recycling office or street-and-sanitation department to ask if they have a recycling plan.

☙ ❧
....

Holidays at work can be fun, but they can also be stressful. If you're not sure whether people in your department exchanges gifts, ask someone who's been there during the holidays.

A holiday party at work (or at home) is a wonderful time to share traditions with people from other cultures. Ask them to bring a traditional dish and allow time for each to talk about their holiday customs.

....

Don't be fooled by the party atmosphere at work. No matter how festive, this isn't the time to confess secrets or criticize the company.

ဢ ©

If your kids get you out of bed at the crack of dawn on the Big Day, you may be able to sleep a little later if you try one of these ideas. On Christmas Eve, show them a festive holiday ribbon and let them watch you tie it to the knob on their bedroom door. Tell them that if they wake up in the morning and the ribbon is still there, it's too early to wake you up. If the ribbon is gone, it's okay to come get you. Remove the ribbon when you get up.

Another idea is to tell them they can open presents in their stockings when they wake up. If you use enough tape on the gifts, unwrapping them can keep kids busy quite awhile.

ဢ ©

Remember that there are ways to celebrate the holidays even if you're away from home:

♦ Treat yourself to a long phone call to someone special.
♦ Treat yourself to a wonderful dinner, a concert or play.
♦ Buy a special little tree. Make ornaments from whatever you can find: cut paper ornaments or snowflakes, make paper chains, string popcorn, make tissue-paper flowers.
♦ Pick a time and tell someone special you'll think of him or her then.
♦ Look for local shelters that need help serving food.

ဢ ©

There's a nice story from Carl Hooper, a pilot for Northwest Airlines, who knows how lonely it can be to be away from home for the holidays.

The Best Christmas Ever

During one Christmas Eve flight, he learned that a new attendant on his flight was sad because she was missing her family's huge annual Christmas Eve dinner for the first time.

Carl realized that their route was directly over the girl's home and he had an idea. He called the attendant into the cockpit, explained his idea and asked for her parents' phone number. He contacted flight services and asked them to call the girl's parents, let them know she would be passing overhead at 33,000 feet soon and ask them if they would go outside in a few minutes.

When the plane passed over the attendant's hometown, he turned on all the aircraft's exterior lights, flashed them a couple of times and asked flight services to wish the family a Merry Christmas from their daughter and the rest of the crew.

A couple of days later, the attendant told Carl how much his thoughtfulness and creativity meant to her and her family and thanked him once again. Says Carl, "I then knew [the attendant] and I both had just experienced the true meaning of Christmas."

※ ※ ※

Maybe you've considered going away for the holidays but figure it's just too difficult to book space at some of the more popular destinations—especially at the last minute. Sometimes, however, it's possible to get reservations because of cancellations, so give it a try! Here are some places that have something special to offer for the holidays. If you can't get in this year, book for next year.

※ ※ ※

Every night from Thanksgiving through January, towns on the route of the 100-mile Starflake Trail in east-central Illinois dazzle visitors with colorful light displays. The way is marked through dark countryside between several communities by "starflake" lights that hang from utility poles. Some of the popular places to stay are historic monuments—many offer spectacular light displays right on the grounds, all boast festive decorations. Besides the lights, visitors come to the area looking for unique gifts in these Amish towns.

For information, contact the Lake Shelbyville Visitors Association (800) 874-3529; the Decatur Area Convention & Visitors Bureau (800) 331-4479, Arthur Visitors Information Center (800) 722-6474 and Arcola Chamber of Commerce, (217) 268-4530.

❀ ❀ ❀

For a very traditional Christmas, try Williamsburg, Virginia. Colonial Williamsburg is the largest historical restoration in the country, and during the three weeks of celebrations, townspeople stroll the streets in eighteenth-century costumes. Madrigal singers, mimes, fifers and drummers entertain. Nearly 200 period homes, shops and taverns have been restored and streets are lighted by lanterns.

Special events include scenes from period plays, baronial balls and the sounds of muskets being fired on December 24 to usher in Christmas (as eighteenth-century Virginians did) just before a huge tree in Market Square is lit with hundreds of white lights. Other celebrations include narrated tours around the Palace Green, instruction in the minuet, banquets and candlelight organ concerts.

For more information call 800-HISTORY. For information and admission cards to attend Holy Eucharist services on Christmas Eve, call (804) 229-2891.

❀ ❀ ❀

Celebrate Christmas at Opryland in Nashville. Enjoy lights, decorations, food and special entertainment—and the country's largest Nativity scene—late November till the end of December. For information, call (615) 889-6611.

❀ ❀ ❀

For a Christmas in Mark Twain's America, The Delta Queen Steamboat Company offers a variety of cruises: Southern Steamboatin' Christmas offers a cruise along the lower Mississippi; Dickens on the Strand cruises the Intercoastal Waterway; Country Christmas explores the waters between New Orleans, Memphis and Nashville. For information, see your travel agent or call (800) 543-1949.

The Best Christmas Ever

* * *

Rockford, Illinois is a Swedish town 85 miles northwest of Chicago that puts up light displays right after Thanksgiving and hosts Christmas festivities each weekend through December 17. Scandinavian decorations woven from straw hang from doorways, and restaurants offer traditional Swedish foods. For more information, contact the Rockford Area Convention & Visitors Bureau, (800) 521-0849.

* * *

Christmas in Natchez, Mississippi, is a time to tour antebellum and Victorian homes, enjoy carriage rides, and attend performances of *The Nutcracker* and special programs at local churches. For more information, call (800) 99-NATCHEZ.

* * *

Nevada City (60 miles northeast of Sacramento) is a gold rush town that attracts visitors year 'round, but hosts Victorian Christmas celebrations in December. Call the Nevada City Chamber of Commerce, (916) 265-2692 for more information.

* * *

In Philadelphia, Fairmount Park House Christmas Tours give you a look at seven historic houses, all decorated for the holidays in themes of old-fashioned Christmases. Some of the houses are lighted as they were in the eighteenth-century. Call (215) 684-7926 for more information.

* * *

"Dickens of a Christmas," the second weekend of December in Franklin, Tennessee, claims to be one of the top 20 tourist events in the Southeast. Talk with Dickens characters as they stroll the streets, take a (free) horse and carriage ride, enjoy old-fashioned music and refreshments. Or, visit the "living windows"—store windows that feature men and women in Victorian clothing demonstrating crafts of that age such as doll-making, carving, pottery-making and weaving. Join in the candlelight caroling party. For information, call (615) 791-9924.

❄ ❄ ❄

Holland, Michigan, is a Dutch community 40 miles southwest of Grand Rapids that celebrates Christmas with lights and old-country atmosphere. Some of the popular places to stay are filled with Victorian antiques. Visitors buy hand-painted wooden shoes and delftware porcelain. For more information, contact the Holland Convention & Visitors Bureau, (616) 396-4221.

❄ ❄ ❄

New Ulm, Minnesota, 75 miles southwest of the Twin Cities, reflects its strong German heritage in its gift shops filled with beer steins and gnomes. Holiday celebration begins late November with the Parade of Lights. On St. Nicholas Day (December 6), everyone gathers at the armory to greet St. Nick and Krumpus, who give fruit and nuts to children who have been good. Three times daily people gather around the Glockenspiel as its 37 bells chime and a door opens on a lighted nativity scene. For more information, contact New Ulm Convention & Visitors Bureau, (507) 354-4217.

❄ ❄ ❄

In Santa Fe, where Christmas lights take the shape of chili peppers and luminarias line dark pathways, a Christmas Eve walk in the Canyon Road district has become a tradition. Enjoy galleries, sing carols, sip hot chocolate or cider. For information, contact the Visitors Bureau, (505) 984-6760.

❄ ❄ ❄

If your idea of a white Christmas is white sand instead of snow, Pensacola, in southeastern Florida, may be the place for you. Christmas in Pensacola offers a variety of events that include boat and street parades, Wild Lights at the Zoo exhibition and more. Call the Convention and Visitor Information Center at (800) 874-1234.

Pensacola also hosts a "First Night" New Year's Eve party, a non-alcoholic event with fun for the entire family. Call (904) 434 2724.

The Best Christmas Ever

* * *

Honolulu has a spectacular display of lights in the downtown municipal area of King Street between Bishop and Alapai streets (as if you needed another reason to visit paradise). Lights go on every evening at 6:30 p.m. from December 2 through January 1. Check the daily newspaper once you're there for other programs and events.

* * *

If spending the holidays on the Caribbean appeals to you, Windjammer Barefoot Cruises has a special Christmas sailing—but you may need to book now for next year. Shipmates are free to join the crew hoisting a sail or steering the ship. Or you can simply relax. Windjammer supports the islands they sail to by purchasing food locally and by responding with aid and equipment during island emergencies. For information, call (800) 327-2600.

> "We need time to dream, time to remember, and time to reach the infinite. We need time to be.
>
> *Gladys Taber, American writer*

Many people experience post-holiday letdown regardless of whether they've had a good holiday, and if that happens to you or someone else in your family, it may help you to know that it's actually a pretty normal response.

But the celebrations don't have to end abruptly. Let your holidays include traditions that continue after the last present has been opened.

♦ Go to the movies Christmas night. There are usually lots of new releases trying to capture an Oscar.

♦ Plan a day-after tradition with friends. Have a potluck with leftover foods.

♦ Rent a video. For the kids: *Andre, Milo and Otis, The Black Stallion, A Charlie Brown Christmas, The Muppet Christmas Carol,* any of the videos of Dr. Seuss, The Berenstain Bears or Barney. For grown ups: *Miracle on 34th Street, It's a Wonderful Life, The Nutcracker, Cool Runnings, City Slickers, The Gods Must Be Crazy, It's a Mad, Mad, Mad, Mad World.*

♦ On Christmas night, have an indoor camping trip right in your living room, complete with sleeping bags, hot chocolate and roasted marshmallows. Turn off the lights and use candles and flashlights. Roast hot dogs in the fireplace.

♦ Save one last gift, maybe something homemade, to give the day after Christmas.

♦ Invite friends to come for cookies and coffee after Christmas. The house will still be clean and it'll give you something to look forward to after all the festivities have ended.

♦ Have a New Year's Eve party with the kids. If you're brave, invite other families and their kids.

♦ Keep Christmas cards displayed through January and send loving thoughts to one person each day.

♦ Make taking down your tree a celebration. Wrap small candy bars in colored tissue paper and hang as ornaments to be eaten at the last minute. Bake a cake and serve as the ornaments are put away.

♦ Go away after the big celebration. Decorations will still be up in most towns, and places may be less crowded.

‟ ‘’

....

What're you doing New Year's Eve? That's the big question once Christmas has passed. In some communities there's a fun alternative to the usual parties or staying home. It's called First Night Celebrations, and it's a great way for the whole family to enjoy ushering in the new year. It's also a great way to be with people if you're alone. The celebrations take the form of huge block parties, starting in the afternoon and lasting until the new year has been ushered in with a spectacular fireworks display. Activities vary from one town to another but follow a basic format. During the day, artists display their work outdoors, a children's festival takes place in the afternoon and is followed by a procession of giant puppets and artists and musicians who invite the children to join in.

In the evening, a variety of performances include dance, music, mime, storytelling, theater, poetry, film, video, multi-media and multi-cultural programs. The price of admission and a button to wear while you wander is under $10, and is generally free for children.

First Night Celebrations started 15 years ago in Boston, and now there are more than 50 communities that host such events. The non-profit organization's objectives are to build a sense of community through a shared cultural experience, broaden and deepen the public's appreciation of the visual and performing arts, make the arts accessible and affordable to everyone, promote an appreciation of cultural diversity and provide an alcohol-free alternative to traditional New Year's Eve parties.

If there isn't a listing in your telephone directory for First Night, call directory assistance, ask the community events editor at your local newspaper or call (617) 542-6111.

"People are always good company when they are doing what they really enjoy."

Samuel Butler, English author

Applaud others. Applaud yourself.

Give joyously. Receive joyously, too.

Chapter 4

Angels among us

and people who demonstrate the spirit of the holidays all year 'round

"There are two ways of spreading light: to be the candle or the mirror that reflects it."

Edith Wharton

Christmas is a time for angels—on greeting cards and wrapping paper, in holiday movies and on tree tops. It's also time when we hear about *human* angels, people who give their time, money or both to help others less fortunate than they. Most never expect to be rewarded and, in fact, are surprised when stories about their generosity become widely known.

Some of these angels do most of their work at Christmas, but many demonstrate the holiday spirit all year.

℘ ℂ℞

Carol and Hurt Porter, founders of Kid-Care, Inc., help feed some of Houston's neediest children. One day Carol was shocked to see a group of neighborhood children eating out of a McDonald's dumpster. After talking it over, she and her husband decided to adopt the kids in that apartment complex—all 125 of them! That led to the creation of Kid-Care and today, with a group of up to 25 volunteers (and no government money), they deliver 18,000 free meals a month directly to children who may only have that one meal to look forward to.

৯৩ ঙ্গ

When Linda Bremner's young son was diagnosed with cancer, cards and letters from family and friends helped him stay cheerful. Once home from the hospital, though, the mail stopped coming and Andy thought nobody cared. Linda became Andy's secret pal, sending him cards and gifts anonymously. Sometimes getting mail made the difference between whether he had a good day or a bad day. Even after Andy figured out who his secret pal was, both kept up the game for four years without acknowledging the fact.

When Andy died, Linda wrote to friends he had made at a camp for children with cancer. The response was so overwhelming she kept writing, then enlisted volunteers. Today she and her volunteers see that 1,100 children who are seriously ill get one piece of mail each week. Each gets a Christmas gift twice a year, in December and July.

৯৩ ঙ্গ

It's a family affair in Arizona. Anne Vinson has contributed hundreds of hours as a volunteer at the Sedona Public Library and Bob Vinson was recently named Volunteer of the Year at Red Rock State Park in Sedona. An electronics engineer before retiring, Bob has devoted hundreds of hours each year doing whatever needed to be done, from pruning fruit trees to designing and installing a new underground watering system, from designing and building a transporter that takes the park's large telescope from storage to the viewing site, to creating a wilderness marsh area, from giving seminars on composting to hosting bird walks.

လ ဃ

For more than 30 years Michael Greenberg, who died in 1995, played Santa to the homeless in Manhattan's infamous Bowery. Carrying a bag of warm gloves, he wandered the gritty neighborhood looking for people who had given up, people who were old, weary, cold.

"Take them, please, they're free, they're a gift," he'd say timidly, dangling a pair of gloves in front of a man or woman who no longer expected kindness from anyone. Then he'd shake his or her hand, an act of communion that Michael said almost invariably brought a smile to their face.

> *"Those who bring sunshine to the lives of others cannot keep it from themselves."*
>
> *Sir James Matthew Barrie,*
> *Scottish playwright and novelist*

Companies can be angels, too, and Coats for Kids is an annual drive initiated by KDLT-TV in Sioux Falls, South Dakota, that collects winter coats and jackets for needy children and adults. The entire community supports this campaign, which runs for five weeks from early October into November, donating thousands of outgrown or unused coats each year. Kmart stores serve as drop-off depots and the Salvation Army picks up and distributes the clothing free through its thrift store.

လ ဃ

In 1991, Richard Baxley, M.D., saw his long hours of work pay off as the doors opened to the Health Care Center for the Homeless, a free, full-service health care clinic in Orlando. It began modestly as a one-night-a-week, one-room clinic serving approximately 15 people each week. The Center's volunteer staff now includes 17 doctors, 40 nurses and 40 specialists, who treat 20 to 40 people each night.

The Best Christmas Ever

෨ ෬

In 1987, Marvin Arrington and his wife, Reneé, restaurant owners in a low-income neighborhood in Greenville, North Carolina, noticed that after school, local kids hung out in front of the restaurant for lack of anything better to do. Greenville's a rough neighborhood, known for substance abuse, crime and violence, but the kids' parents have low-paying jobs and so childcare is out of the question.

Marvin began inviting the kids into the restaurant to get help with their homework. He sometimes offered them personal guidance, too. Pretty soon, so many kids were showing up that they overcrowded the restaurant, so he and Reneé rented a building nearby and established the Little Willie Center. Parents, teachers, local church members and students from East Carolina University were recruited to run the new tutoring and mentoring program. The Little Willie Center is so popular that kids asked to attend on weekends and holidays, so Marvin organized weekend sports and educational activities, too.

෨ ෬

Traci Taylor was only 6 when she was diagnosed with leukemia. She was in and out of hospitals fighting for her life until she was 10 and received a bone-marrow transplant. One of the few things she had to look forward to in the hospital was the "toy train," a cart that was wheeled through the children's ward with puzzles, books and dolls that she could borrow to play with.

As a young teen, Traci was hospitalized in a new town and discovered it didn't have a toy train so she decided to supply one. Her father, brother and some friends from her church built the train according to her specifications and her mother asked shopkeepers for donations.

That was in 1992 and the train continues to make its daily rounds. Once a week she is the volunteer who brings it around. Her goal is to expand the service to other local hospitals.

ℰ ℭ

Julia Goldstein was 91 when she sat in on her great-grandson's first-grade class and saw bored children folding paper airplanes or staring out the window. After 60 years as a professional educator specializing in early childhood development, she had some opinions. One of them was that these kids needed more attention than they were getting in a crowded classroom or from working parents who didn't have the time or energy to take an active interest in schoolwork.

Julia decided to remedy the situation and founded "Partners for Educational Excellence," which pairs seniors with first-graders who aren't doing well in school. After selling the superintendent of her local school district on the plan and getting the names of 10 first-graders who would have trouble advancing to second grade, she got parental approval and then recruited volunteers to work with the children one-on-one, half an hour, one day a week.

The seniors weren't specially trained, but they cared about kids. And the first year, their efforts resulted in the promotion of eight of the 10 at-risk kids.

ℰ ℭ

In 1993, residents in the town of Billings, Montana (pop. 80,000) stood up against a group of white supremacy terrorists to protect the religious freedom of its Jewish families.

Threats against Tammie Schnitzer started in 1989, when she volunteered to host a meeting of Montana's Jewish families. One morning a threat came over the phone: "Stop or we'll make you stop," the voice warned. Later that day, someone threw something at her minivan, breaking one of the windows.

In the years that followed, fliers that attacked Jews and homosexuals were often thrown on driveways throughout Billings. Ku Klux Klan newspapers spread messages of hate, and skinheads showed up to harass worshipers at a church attended by African-American residents.

During this time, Margaret MacDonald, part-time director of the Montana Association of Churches, circulated a petition that opposed hatred and bigotry, but town leaders were wary of signing because they felt that the less said, the better. But as the attacks escalated, so did Margaret's insistence that something be done. Eventually, other Billings residents began to take action, some of them attending services at the African Methodist Episcopal Wayman Chapel as a show of solidarity against skinheads who showed up there.

Then on the evening of Dec. 2, 1993, Tammie and her husband, Brian, were startled by the crash of glass breaking in their son's bedroom. They ran in to find that a cinder block had been thrown through the window with such force that it had sailed across the room and flattened the stuffed animals on Isaac's bed. Tattered pieces of the paper menorah, which had been taped to the window earlier that evening, lay among the pieces of glass. Fortunately, Isaac hadn't been in the room at the time.

When Margaret found out about the attack, she suggested to her minister that they support the Jewish families by copying pictures of menorahs and letting the children color them at Sunday School. Other local churches agreed to do the same thing. That week hundreds of menorahs appeared in the windows of Christian homes in Billings.

On Dec. 7, *The Billings Gazette* published a full-page menorah that readers could cut out and tape on a window. Local businesses also distributed copies of menorahs. Within a few weeks, nearly 6,000 homes in Billings had menorahs on display.

Everyone who displayed the menorah was at risk of being a target of hate. The violence didn't end immediately, but eventually the hate literature disappeared and the attacks stopped. Perhaps the supremacists got the message when someone rented a billboard to say, "Not in Our Town! No Hate. No Violence. Peace on Earth."

℘ ℛ
....

Over the last 10 years, Marion Crook has been mom-away-from-home to more than 500 West Point Military Academy cadets. They

....

may be homesick or stressed out, or maybe they just want to sleep late in the morning. So Marion and her husband, Lee, have opened their four-bedroom home in Fishkill, New York to any cadets who show up. When the beds are full, she hands out pillows and blankets and their guests sleep on the floor.

ഇ ര

Bessie Baughn is an angel who delivers free VCRs and videos to terminal patients, and toys to kids who are undergoing chemotherapy. This is her gift to the people of San Bruno, California. She also organizes charity fairs, anti-drug programs and outings for seniors. To pay for it, she mortgaged her house. She ignores the fact that she's had two strokes, back surgery and injuries from a car accident.

ഇ ര

Rhea Joseph has visited Christmas tree lots in Norfolk, Virginia every November for the last three years to ask the proprietor if he or she could donate a tree to help make the holiday complete for a needy military family. When she finds willing donors, Rhea delivers the trees to the families herself, with a food basket and gifts for the children.

ഇ ര

In 1988, Days Inn, at its headquarters in Atlanta, started recruiting homeless people from shelters to work in its reservations department. Since the program started, Days Inn has hired more than 40 homeless people, providing job training and often providing them with rooms at the Inn at a nominal fee until they find permanent housing.

ഇ ര

Hotels/Motels in Partnership is a nationwide nonprofit program that puts individual hotels together with charitable agencies. Hotels and motels that participate in the program offer shelter to battered spouses who need a place to stay to escape violence at home. More than 800 hotels and motels in 46 states have agreed to donate lodging.

ഇ ❧

In 1990, Arby's launched a pilot program at its Atlanta headquarters to give jobs to the homeless. It started by hiring five women from the ACHOR Center in Atlanta. Arby's supplied training, uniforms, shoes and monthly transportation passes. When the women saved half the money they needed for housing, Arby's matched it and ACHOR helped them find apartments.

ഇ ❧

At Little Caesars Love Kitchen foundation, based in Detroit, Michigan, corporate and franchise employees have volunteered in two mobile pizza restaurants that have served nearly 900,000 homeless people at 1,900 locations in 425 cities.

"Example is not the main thing in influencing others—it is the only thing."

Albert Schweitzer

In 1989, John Foster and Eddie Staton brought 18 other African-American men together to form MAD DADS (Men Against Destruction Defending Against Drugs and Social Disorder), to help troubled youngsters in North Omaha, Nebraska. Their goal was to be positive role models, disrupt drug sales, lower incidences of violence and help the neighborhood kids learn to get along better. The campaign was launched as 75 men took to the streets in MAD DADS hats and T-shirts, with buckets of paint and a mission to cover gang graffiti.

MAD DADS has grown to more than 900 members who often find themselves serving as surrogate fathers and offering street counseling to kids in need. They do whatever else is needed, from providing midnight street patrols to making presentations to local schools, service clubs and community organizations, from confronting drug dealers and counseling gang members to acting as chaperons at community events.

In cooperation with the Omaha Police Department, MAD DADS cosponsored a gun buy-back program that took in more than 2,500 guns. They also buy back toy guns for $1 each to discourage violence.

ꕤ ꕤ

For Frank and Janet Ferrel, being angels started with giving a blanket and a pillow to a homeless man. Their son Trevor was shocked to learn that there were people who had to sleep on steam vents in downtown Philadelphia to stay warm. That first gift led them to making regular visits in their van, bringing food and clothing to the neighborhood's homeless.

Soon others heard about what they were doing and offered to help. Now more than 70 local families cook meals for the project, a McDonald's donates burgers, fish sandwiches and apple pies. A 30-room house was donated to the project, which Frank, Janet and other volunteers remodeled and repaired to use as a shelter.

ꕤ ꕤ

After being a Big Brother for 11 years, John Schleck of Minneapolis-St. Paul, Minnesota became a Little Brother to help people over 65 who are alone.

ꕤ ꕤ

Thora Shaw is called "Mom" by the inmates at the County Jail in Jasper, Missouri, where she's visited for nearly 20 years. It started when she visited one inmate and was later asked by a guard to talk to another prisoner about some problems he was having. Thora offers inmates her friendship and encouragement and even counsels them on their personal problems. Twice each week, she assists with adult education classes and has helped 40 inmates obtain GEDs. Like any good mom, she's also willing to give haircuts for free.

ᴈᴑ ᴄᴙ

At its 1990 convention in New Orleans, the Professional Convention Management Association launched a "Feed the Needy" program to donate the unserved meals to a shelter for the homeless. During the four-day convention the extra meals fed nearly 5,000 people.

ᴈᴑ ᴄᴙ

At Yale, more than 2,200 students volunteer to work in soup kitchens or tutor ghetto kids. At Rice, a quarter of the students volunteer. A sorority at Howard University in Washington tutors children in a public-housing shelter near the campus. A survey of 67 colleges and universities showed that one of four undergraduates volunteers in the community.

ᴈᴑ ᴄᴙ

Over the years, Nils and Jan Anderson have collected a staggering $311,000 to benefit the Animal Humane Society of Hennepin County, Minnesota. Most of what they've collected has been in small door-to-door donations of $5 to $30.

ᴈᴑ ᴄᴙ

Grandma, Please is a volunteer group of seniors in the Chicago area who stay at home from 3 p.m. to 6 p.m. one day a week so kids can call them after school. Most kids go home to an empty house and "Grandma" gives them someone to check in with who will talk to them about school and maybe even help with homework.

ℰℛ ℭℛ

As executive director of Hawaii's Homeless Women and Children Crisis Intervention, Laree Wartena, has many opportunities to be an angel, but one of her favorite memories occurred at Christmastime. At 3 a.m., three days before Christmas, she got a call from a girl in Waikiki who said she'd been beaten up and was hiding.

When the girl got to the shelter, she was a mess. She said she was 21, but Laree says she looked more like 18. Usually people stay in Laree's home for a few days before they move to the shelter so they're more comfortable—that's how this girl ended up with the Wartena family for Christmas.

"My kids had gone through their things looking for gifts they could give to the girl so she'd have some presents. After she'd opened them, I asked if there wasn't someone in her family she could call who would help. She said she'd left home and a troubled mother when she was 13, and hadn't been back since. She finally admitted that her dad had always wanted her to stay with him, but she had never felt good enough about herself to take him up on his offer. She agreed to call, though, and while they were on the phone, her dad talked her into going to live with him in Canada.

"That was good news, but then her dad wanted to talk to me. 'Thank you so much,' he said. 'My baby is coming home and she's going back to school.' I was very happy for both of them and that was my best Christmas ever."

> "Loneliness and the feeling of being
> unwanted is the most terrible poverty."
>
> Mother Teresa

Dream dreams. Celebrate miracles.

Reach out. Go inside, too.

Chapter 5

You can make a difference, too

*"I am he, as you are he, as you are me,
and we are all together."*

John Lennon and Paul McCartney

Maybe it's been in the back of your mind that you'd like to make more of a contribution to others. And you tell yourself you will, once you get some of your bills paid off. Or you vow that once you complete this project or that, *then* you'll have time to volunteer. But if you're like me, there will always be bills waiting to be paid. I've recognized that never in this lifetime will I actually have a time *between* projects.

But while I was writing this book, I began to recognize ways I can make small contributions almost daily. I realized that volunteering my time has to *be* one of my projects rather than something I try to squeeze in between them.

If you've been considering contributing to charities or volunteering your skills, Christmas is a perfect time to start. If you have the time and energy for a grand effort, go for it!

If you'd like to help but have limited time or money, that's okay, too. Drop change into the collection jars on store counters that invite you to contribute to the March of Dimes, Ronald McDonald Houses, charities to feed the children and other causes you believe in. When markets offer to help schools purchase computers in exchange for donated cash register receipts, take the time to donate yours. If you see kids washing cars as a fund-raising event and your car needs to be washed, let the kids do it. Drop some change into the Salvation Army kettle. Help an elderly neighbor do yard work. Volunteer to deliver Meals on Wheels or drive blind folks to doctor's appointments. Volunteer to be a teacher's helper at an elementary school or work with your local Red Cross.

Here are some other groups that would appreciate your help:

♦ Make-a-Wish Foundation of America grants the wishes of children under 18 who are terminally ill. To donate money or volunteer your time, contact your local agency or 4601 N. 16th St., Suite 205, Phoenix, AZ 85016. (800) 722-WISH.

♦ Carol and Hurt Porter, founders of Kid-Care, Inc., help feed some of Houston's neediest children. Send contributions to Box 92025, Houston, TX 77206. (800) 566-0084.

♦ Special Olympics International provides sports training and athletic competition in a variety of Olympic-type sports for mentally retarded children and adults. It accepts donations and needs volunteers to work during the sport competitions. 1350 New York Ave. NW, Suite 500, Washington, D.C. 20005. (202) 628-3630.

♦ Marvin and Reneé Arrington, founders of the Little Willie Center, an after-school tutoring and monitoring program for kids, rely on donations to keep the program running. P.O. Box 20191, Greenville, NC. Call (919) 752-9083 before 2 p.m. or after 5 p.m. EST.

♦ Hawaii's Homeless Women and Children Crisis Intervention shelters homeless women and children. Contact Laree Wartena, Box 1587, Waianae, HI 96702. (808) 696-2406.

◆ Trevor's Campaign provides food and clothing to the homeless. Contact Frank and Janet Ferrel, Resources for Human Development, 3415 Westchester Pike, Newtown, PA, 18940. (610) 325-0640.

◆ Childhelp USA, in conjunction with Foresters National, offers a 24-hour hotline for young victims and those who abuse them. 6463 Independence Ave., Woodland Hills, CA 91367. (800) 4-A-CHILD for emergency calls, (818) 347-7280 if you have questions.

◆ The Sunshine Foundation fulfills the dreams of terminally and chronically ill children. 2001 Bridge St., Philadelphia, PA 19124. (215) 535-1413.

◆ Child Find of America has located nearly 3,000 missing children, most of whom have been abducted by a parent. Its mission is to help parents who cannot afford private detectives and haven't found their children through police efforts. P.O. Box 277, New Paltz, NY. (800) I-AM-LOST.

◆ Habitat for Humanity, International uses donated money, material and labor to construct housing for qualified individuals who, in turn, must participate in the construction of their own and other Habitat homes. Contact 419 W. Church St., Americus, GA 31709. (912) 924-6935.

◆ The Hole in the Wall Gang Camp Fund offers camping experiences to children 7 to 17 who are physically incapacitated or suffering from severe illness. 555 Long Wharf Dr., New Haven, CT 96511. (203) 772-0522.

◆ Big Brothers/Big Sisters of America recruits men and women to spend time with children who don't have positive male or female adult role models. To donate or volunteer, contact your local agency or 230 North 13th St., Philadelphia, PA 19197. (215) 567-7000.

◆ Children's Defense Fund acts as an advocate for the rights of children, primarily the poor, minority and handicapped. 122 C St. NW, Washington, D.C. 20001. (202) 628-8787.

- Feed the Children provides food, clothing, educational materials, medical equipment and other necessities to people who lack them because of famine, drought, flood, war or poverty. Last year, people contributed more than 3,500 handmade Christmas stockings and love boxes to FTC's "Christmas 4 Kids" program. These were distributed to children who might otherwise have had nothing for the holidays. P.O. Box 36, Oklahoma City, OK 73101. (405) 942-0228.

- Reading is Fundamental has put more than 93 million books into the hands of children through schools, libraries, community centers, shelters and hospitals. Smithsonian Institution, 600 Maryland Ave. SW, Suite 500, Washington, D.C. (202) 287-3220.

- Linda Bremner is committed to sending one piece of mail each week and Christmas presents twice a year to 1,100 seriously ill children. If you'd like to help, send letters and cards with a friendly message in an *unsealed* envelope (unaddressed and inside your mailing envelope). Make salutations generic and do not send cards or messages that mention getting well (some kids know they won't), or religious sentiments. Unwrapped gifts and postage stamps are appreciated, too. Send to Linda Bremner, Love Letters, Inc., Box 416875, Chicago, IL 60641 or call 708-620-1970.

- National Committee for Prevention of Child Abuse acts to prevent child abuse in all its forms. 332 S. Michigan Ave., Suite 950, Chicago, IL 60604. (312) 663 3520.

"Trust your heart...Never deny it a hearing.
It is the kind of house oracle that often
foretells the most important.

Balthasar Gracian

Some wild animal groups offer to let you "adopt" one of their own. For a specific donation, you'll receive a certificate and maybe even a picture.

Adopt an orca through the Whale Museum, (206) 378-4710; a gray through the Tarlton Foundation, (415) 433-3163; a dolphin through Oceanic Society, (415) 441-1106; or a wolf through Wolf Haven International, (800) 448-9653. Adopt a favorite animal at your local zoo.

If you'd like to adopt an acre of South American rain forest you can, through The Nature Conservancy, (800) 628-6860 or the Rainforest Action Network, (415) 398-4404.

❋ ❋ ❋

For a copy of the *National Green Pages,* which identifies businesses dedicated to making a difference, contact Co-Op America, 1850 M St. NW, Suite 700, Washington, D.C. 20036, (202) 872-5307. The cost is $5.95 plus $1 for shipping.

❋ ❋ ❋

The Holiday Project has more than 1,100 volunteers in 411 communities in 28 states, who visit nearly 11,000 people during the holiday season. Volunteers visit people confined in hospitals, nursing homes and prisons to offer companionship. To donate or volunteer, contact your local Holiday Project or contact Sally Cooney, the Holiday Project, P.O. Box 6347, Lake Worth, FL 33466. (407) 966-5702.

❋ ❋ ❋

Christmas in April★U.S.A. is a national agency that recruits volunteers to help low-income elderly and disabled homeowners by tackling sagging roofs, leaky pipes, peeling paint, rotting steps and other health and safety hazards. Once a year, volunteers both skilled and unskilled, make home repairs for seniors who have been unable to afford or make themselves. The program now supports more than 300 groups; in 1994, more than 120,000 men, women and children rehabilitated 4,000 homes and nonprofit facilities.

To make a donation or volunteer, look in your phone book under Christmas in April and the name of your town, or write 1225 Eye St. NW, Suite 601, Washington, D.C. 20005. (202) 326-8268.

* * *

For more ideas (like starting a Midnight Basketball League to give inner-city kids something to do), read *You Can Change America,* published by Earthworks Group and available through bookstores or directly from Earthworks Press, 1400 Shattuck Ave., #25, Berkeley, CA 94705. (510) 841-5866. $5.95.

* * *

If your community has a problem, chances are the Community Action Network (CAN) has a whole booklet of solutions that have been tried and proven successful in other communities. Leaders in the advertising and media field felt that too many good solutions to community problems are rarely known beyond the communities where they originate, so they decided to develop a databank to collect and share solutions with other communities.

The 20 booklet titles include: AIDS, Alcohol Abuse, Child Abuse, Criminal Justice, Drug Abuse, Drunk Driving, Education, Elderly Care, Environment, Family Concerns, Handicapped, Homeless, Housing, Hunger, Medical Care, Missing Children, Rape, Street Crime, Teenage Suicide and Unemployment. Booklets are available from CAN, 211 E. 43rd St., Suite 1203, New York, NY 10017. They cost $5 for the first booklet and $3 for each additional booklet, or you can buy all 20 for $50.

ℰℴ ℭℛ

If you have a project in mind but aren't sure how to go about starting up, the Points of Light Foundation, a program initiated during the Bush administration, offers these tips:

- ◆ You don't have to do a project all by yourself.
- ◆ Don't try everything at once.

- Examine the problem closely, see what's being done, start with one step at a time.
- Have a vision about what you want to accomplish, but be reasonable.
- You may not be able to feed the world, but maybe you can contribute to easing the hunger problems in one neighborhood.
- Involve others—from work, church, community organizations.
- Be visible. Find ways to let people know you're there.

★

*"I am
only one,
But still I am one.
I cannot do everything,
But still I can do something;
And because I cannot do everything
I will not refuse to do the something that
I can do."*

❀❀❀

❀❀❀

*Edward Everett Hale's pledge to the
Lend-a-Hand Society*

Chapter 6

Meditations for the holidays

The dictionary defines the word "meditate" as thinking contemplatively. We do that more than we realize, but most of the time we meditate about our frustrations, fears, lacks and limitations. What we focus on expands, and so when we think about the things we *don't* want in our lives, we actually create more of them.

The reason guided meditations are so popular is because they seem to reach a part of us that knows we can be calm, capable and peaceful. There's a part of us that knows it's better to slow down and enjoy family and friends rather than rushing from one busy project to another. There's a part of us that knows that people are more important than things and that we deserve everything we truly want.

When you read the following meditations, read them contemplatively. Slow down. Notice what you're thinking. Notice what you're feeling. Enjoy.

Slowing down

Sometimes it seems like we're so busy doing things that have to be done that we don't have time to do the things we *want* to do. We promise ourselves that once we finish this and accomplish that, *then* we'll slow down. But we don't. Instead, we find more things that need to be done.

Slowing down isn't always easy, maybe because we've let ourselves be convinced that when we're busy, we're responsible, efficient and worthy of praise. And during the holidays, we try to add *more* to an already busy schedule. But we were not put here on earth to see how many lists of tasks we could complete and how fast we could get them done. The part of us that knows the truth whispers to us at quiet moments: We are here to enjoy the gifts in our lives, the love of our family and friends, the beauty of the sunset, the perfection of a rose. We're here to learn about ourselves and each other and God.

It's okay just to sit and appreciate the beauty of a Christmas tree; it's okay to listen to the carolers a little longer. It's okay to take a long walk through the park and think about what we want from this life and what we want to give. It's okay *not* to always be busy.

I now agree to change my mind about my need to be busy. I slow down, listen to my heart and enjoy my life.

Honesty

Most of us would describe ourselves as honest—we're truthful when someone asks what we do for a living, what books we enjoy and what we think about the President. We tend to be less truthful to ourselves. We often say we don't mind doing someone a favor when, in fact, we mind a great deal. We shrug modestly when someone congratulates us on an accomplishment, saying it was no big thing even if it was. We say nothing's the matter when we are hurt and after a time, we believe it's true.

It's important to tell others the truth and just as important to honor ourselves with the same respect. The holiday season can be a good time to practice. We can let our family know what traditions and celebrations are important to us. We don't have to agree to go to events we don't want to go to. We can say no when we're asked to do more than we comfortably can. When we speak the truth gently, everybody wins.

I accept the challenge to tell myself the truth about what I think and feel and want. I slow down and take cues from my body, which signals me when I forget.

Conflict

Conflict can be frightening—if we were taught that disagreement means someone is right and someone is wrong.

The holiday season can bring conflict because it's a time when we're rushed and full of expectations. Others are rushed and have expectations, too. When we are able to let go of the fear (disguised as anger), we can see conflict for what it really is—two or more ideas where once there was only one.

I accept conflict as a normal part of life and let go of the old responses of anger and fear when someone I care about doesn't agree with what I say, want or do. I now look at conflict as an opportunity to explore new possibilities.

Balance

It's easy to understand the need for balance when we're skiing, skating or riding a bike. If we aren't in balance, we're insecure, we struggle and maybe fall.

It's not as easy to tell when our life is out of balance. But whenever we experience a longing to do or be something different, the small voice of our inner self is nudging us toward balance. It tempts us to linger in a beautiful park, reach out to someone in need, go within for guidance.

I give myself permission to take care of the most important person in my life—me. I accept that I deserve to enjoy my life, and I easily find ways to cut back or eliminate some of my busy work so I have time for more of the things I enjoy. I begin my new life in balance right now.

Joy

Joy, the theme of many Christmas carols, is sometimes a hard emotion to experience. To feel joy, we have to *notice* the event. To notice the event, we have to be moving slowly enough to be aware the moment it happens.

I slow down and notice opportunities for joy: a beautiful sunset, the touch of a child, an unexpected gift from a friend. I look for and find opportunities to bring joy into others' lives, too.

Perfection

Perfection is relative. And subjective. And yet it's easy to get caught up in trying to meet a dozen different peoples' visions of perfection. No wonder we sometimes feel inadequate!

We can make this holiday more enjoyable by letting go of our need to be perfect. We can think of it as a bad habit we once learned that we're now ready to let go of.

I let go of my old belief that I have to be perfect. I understand that I already am perfect, just the way I am and just the way I am not.

Living in the moment

It's easy to be swept from the moment by thoughts of chores that have to be done, especially during the holidays. But when we constantly focus on the future, we miss out on the present. We rush through selecting gifts and wrapping them instead of enjoying what we're doing. We only pay *half* attention to what our children tell us because we're anxious to be doing something that "needs" to be done.

We can learn to live in the moment. It may take time, but it took awhile to learn to do three things at once, too. We may need to give ourselves permission not to be superpeople. We need to remember that it's okay to do one thing at a time. We need to remember that it's okay to have fun and it's okay not to get everything done.

When we remember to live in the moment, we give ourselves an opportunity to get to know ourselves better. We have an opportunity to get to know other people in our lives better, too.

I let go of my belief that I have to plan and plot and rush to ensure that everything gets done. I pay attention to what I am doing at the moment. I look for ways to enjoy what I'm doing. I trust that the things that really need to be done will get done—even if I'm not thinking about them every minute of every day.

Hope

Hope is a gift we give ourselves that reminds us we can always reach our goals. Before anything was created, first it was a thought. What we can imagine, we can accomplish so long as we hold firmly to our desire, choose activities that lead us toward our goals and don't give up.

I know that I deserve to have my heart's desire. I accept opportunities that lead me toward my goal or something even better.

Giving and receiving

If we were raised to believe that it's better to give than to receive, we may have trouble accepting gifts from others. We need to remember that with every gift there is an opportunity to give and receive. As the giver, we receive appreciation from the person we give to. When we are the receiver, we can give the gift of appreciation to the person who gave to us.

I agree to give and receive lovingly.

Patience

Patience is calmly waiting for the natural unfolding of events. Unfortunately, all our training seems to be about accomplishing, rushing, making things happen.

But patience is valuable. A tree only grows as fast as it can grow. A flower blooms when it's ready.

When we try to rush things, we're often successful in terms of getting the project done, but find we've become anxious, frustrated or angry in the process.

When we make a conscious effort to slow down, let things move at their natural pace and *be okay* with them moving at that pace, we take a giant step in the direction of becoming not only more patient, but more peaceful, too.

I give myself permission to be patient. I recognize that it isn't my job to rush everything to completion. I know that when I set things in motion and do whatever is reasonably needed, everything will get done.

Gratitude

It's easy to get caught up in the scramble to have more "stuff." It's easy to feel frustrated with areas of our life that aren't the way we'd like them to be. Yet when we focus on what we don't want, that's what we get—more of what we don't want. Our minds are so powerful that we literally bring things into our lives with our thoughts.

When we remember to be grateful for what we *do* have, we not only become happier, we attract more of what we want into our lives.

I stop several times a day and give thanks for what I have, just the way it is and just the way it is not.

Count your blessings.

Thank your angels.

Talk to God.   Listen.

About the author

Karin Ireland is the author of 10 books, including *The Job Survival Instruction Book,* also published by Career Press. She plans to enjoy the best Christmas ever herself, using this book to help her remember to slow down and make time for the things that are really important.

Index